THE FOUR FROM GILA BEND

Sheriff Bill Ferrine receives a telegram from his friend Burt Anders, sheriff of the neighboring town of Farley, warning that the outlaw Holt Wallace will soon disembark in Stantonsburg from the Arizona Express. According to the message, Wallace is armed and dangerous, with a price on his head of two thousand dollars. When a passenger matching the description steps onto the platform, and responds to Ferrine's warning by pulling a gun on him, the sheriff shoots him dead in self-defense. But something is very wrong. The stranger's draw was uncertain; his gun is an ancient pistol that hasn't been fired in a decade; Anders swears he never sent that telegram. As the two lawmen investigate, it becomes clear that the shot man was no two-thousand-dead-or-alive outlaw, but someone who was set up to be killed . . .

D1649949

THE FOUR FROM GILA BEND

MERLE CONSTINER

SAGEBRUSH
Large Print Westerns

First published in the United States by Ace Books

First Isis Edition
published 2018
by arrangement with
Golden West Literary Agency

A catalogue record for this book is available
from the British Library.

ISBN 978–1–78541–552–4 (pb)

Published by
F. A. Thorpe (Publishing)
Anstey, Leicestershire

Set by Words & Graphics Ltd.
Anstey, Leicestershire
Printed and bound in Great Britain by
T. J. International Ltd., Padstow, Cornwall

This book is printed on acid-free paper

CHAPTER
ONE

Stantonsburg, sometimes called Snakesburg, or simply S-burg, was a small marshaling yard and roundhouse — but pretty insignificant as a cow country county seat. The best you could say for it was that it was honest and struggled along; the worst was that it was too handy for a man on the dodge to drop from a freight car and cool his heels.

It wasn't the meanest place in the Arizona Territory by a long shot, and its sheriff, Bill Ferrine, wasn't a man-hungry killer for the hell of it, but it would have been a mistake to underestimate either of them.

At exactly 8:08 one night, Sheriff Ferrine appeared at the shadowy far end of the depot platform, and waited. He was a big meaty man, almost lumbering in his movements, empty-faced. He dressed in worn range work clothes, because he considered himself a working man, and because he had a wife and two children and felt he shouldn't try to afford anything else. Some sheriffs minted money; he would have knocked down any man who brought up such a touchy subject.

There was thin mist in the night, scarcely enough to dampen the backs of Ferrine's hands, but he could see it standing out smokily before the lamplight of the depot window about twenty feet in front of him. In his pocket was a telegram that his son had brought to him when he had been eating supper, in script, as the stationmaster had taken it down from his instrument: *Holt Wallace two thousand dollars dead or alive getting off Stantonsburg station on 8:12 ankle long yellow slicker at least two guns inside chin strapped big horse blanket safety pin black Stetson wish to say sure don't take no chances with this one* (signed) *Burt*.

Holt Wallace, Holt Wallace, thought Ferrine. *I never heard of him as I recall.*

Burt Anders was sheriff over at Farley, at the foot of the Mazatzals. He was a long-time friend of Ferrine's, and about his closest.

At 8:15 the big bulky iron locomotive of the Arizona Express of the Atlantic & Pacific, wet with mist, coughing steam, chugged in. When it ground out, clinking, clanking, bells ringing, one man alone stood on the platform in the light of the depot window.

A smallish, slightly hunched man, middle aged, in a stiff yellow slicker. One hand held a patterned miniature carpetbag; the other was deep through a pocket slot in his coat. His coat collar was held together by a five inch safety pin.

Ferrine began to walk toward him.

The man said, "Ross? Mike?"

"Just don't move," said Ferrine.

The man said, "You're not Mike Ross."

His hand came out of his slicker pocket with a wallowing sort of a jerk, half catching on the pocket, with a huge old pistol in his fist. Ferrine shot him; and

2

he shot as he always shot, for certain. Rule one in this business was to keep alive.

But in the next split instant, even before the dead man hit the platform, Ferrine had a rush of panic.

The gun the man had come out with wasn't a two thousand-dead-or-alive gun, and it hadn't been drawn by a two thousand-dead-or-alive expert — despite the telegram in Ferrine's pocket.

He didn't know what had happened, but instinct told him he had somehow been trapped. He could feel it in his guts.

An invisible door had shut him into something, and a padlock had clicked in its hasp, fixing him there, and good.

He examined the man's pistol. It was gummy and black with old grease, and hadn't been fired for ten years, surely. Sheriff Ferrine opened the little satchel and laid out its contents: a clean change of collar and cuffs (no change of clean shirt), a tiny deck of cards for solitaire playing to while away the tedium, a chicken sandwich, a dill pickle, a quarter pound wedge of rattrap cheese, and a razor; no soap for the razor, any soap handy would do. The feeling Ferrine got was domesticity and either hardship, or stinginess. He repacked and reclosed the carpetbag.

He turned his attention to the man's person. No moneybelt. There were six dollars in his wallet, a horn comb with broken teeth, a return ticket to Farley, and a membership card in a stockman's association, giving the bearer's name as T. L. Cloud.

Other pockets yielded nothing further.

The skinny little stationmaster was standing beside him.

"I seen it all," said the stationmaster. "He didn't have no call to whip out his weapon thataway, Bill. You spoke to him harmless and civil. Was I standin' in your shoes, I would have did the same thing you done. Pertected myself. You done the right thing, Bill."

Ferrine said nothing.

The stationmaster said, "You kin count on me. I seen it. You done right."

"A sheriff is always right," said Ferrine. "Even when he's wrong."

"You know what I think?" said the stationmaster, trying to hide the falseness of his true belief. "I think maybe he come to town just to gun you."

This was so ridiculous, Ferrine turned his head aside.

The stationmaster said, "That nephew o' mine, Bill, the one convicted for stealing a single-tree, who you got off the county road and put back in a cell because he has T. B., his mother will always be deeply grateful to you for that."

"He was sick," said Ferrine curtly. "Too sick to be swinging a mattock. The deceased's name here is Cloud. Would you do me two favors? Get Mr. Cloud taken to the undertaking parlor, and send someone to Mike Ross and have him meet me at my home right away?"

"O' course, Bill."

"And I've got to get to Farley, immediately. When's the next westbound train?"

4

"This is Wednesday. It comes through here on Saturday at nine-fifty-eight p.m."

"Too late. Much too late."

"Got anything agin ridin' a caboose?"

Ferrine shook his head.

"Three-Nineteen, a fast freight made up in Albuquerque and bound for San Francisco, is due here in exactly two hours. It can drop you off at Farley about two. I kin arrange it with the boys; they'll be glad to do it for you."

Ferrine looked at his watch.

"She'll be through at eleven-twenty-seven," said the stationmaster. "And you better be here. She rolls trailin' smoke and fire."

"I'll be here," said Ferrine.

The Ferrines had a big trunk with tin corners and a battered accordian valise with dry leather straps and rusty buckles, both pieces having been inherited by Annie from her father, who had been a missionary in his youth. They had never used the trunk. Bill had used the valise twice, once to Waco, once to Cheyenne, on both occasions to bring back apprehended prisoners. The first thing Ferrine did when he reached home was to put the valise on the bed, stare at it, and decide not to take it along, that he wouldn't need it. He had told Annie of the incident in the short distance from the front door to the bedroom closet and now she stood watching him in silence. His two sons, fourteen and three, stood watching him, too.

Annie said, "What do you make of it?"

"Somebody wanted him killed," said Ferrine bleakly. "And I obliged."

"Who was he, I wonder? A Mr. Cloud, or this Holt Wallace?"

"Mr. Cloud, I'd guess. I'd say there was no Holt Wallace."

"I wish you'd cool down, Bill," she said. "I don't like to see you with that grayish white around the nostrils."

"The gun I wear is official. It's for official business and official business only. I don't like being juggled."

"I wouldn't much like it either," said William Junior, the fourteen-year-old son. His face showed pale anger, too. In all things he was like his father, and at all times he was one with his father.

"Don't get killed, Bill," said his wife.

"I don't aim to," he said. "But you knew when you married me you were marrying a badge and a percentage."

"I'm glad you're going," she said quietly.

He was just giving her a peck of a goodbye kiss, and reaching for his hat, when Mike Ross knocked at the front door. Ross was a potbellied little man in a gray serge suit, and with a bulbous red veined nose. He was a cattleman, dealing and specializing in good breeder-bulls, good but not deluxe, reasonably priced. He was a rich man, humble, and a loyal friend of the Ferrines.

"I saw the body at the undertaker's," he said.

Ferrine nodded.

"And heard the stationmaster's story, which is already flying around town. The deceased's name is

T. L. Cloud, from up around Farley. I've done a little business with him in the past. I won't say I'm glad he's dead, but I am."

They all looked at him, startled.

"Why?" asked Ferrine.

"He was such a nuisance. He thought you bought a breeder-bull like you bought a horse at a county fair from a stranger. Haggle, haggle. Asking price, selling price, words and argument."

"I'm going to Farley, Mike," said Ferrine.

"Then be careful. Farley isn't any ladies' bazaar like Stantonsburg."

By midnight Ferrine was in the caboose of 319, thundering and swaying westbound, with his destination ninety miles up the track.

CHAPTER
TWO

At two-thirty, Ferrine was combing the streets and side streets of Farley's business section, inquiring about Sheriff Burt Anders, his own badge out of sight under his corduroy vest, saying he'd like to ask him how to get a drunken tramp of a father-in-law out of your house when he had decided to come and camp with you. That always got sympathy and didn't arouse any antagonism. Farley, by nature, was an antagonistic town, especially to people it didn't recognize. Ferrine had gone to Anders' quarters at the courthouse first, of course. Anders wasn't there, but Ferrine had learned he'd find him foot-loosing it around town somewhere, that Anders never went to bed until sunrise. It wasn't until just before dawn, really, that Farley's dives and joints and honky-tonks showed their teeth. The boys of 319 had treated him as one of themselves, and the trip from Stantonsburg had been surprisingly pleasant.

It was at a place called *McGuire's*, a hole-in-the-wall eatery, that he found his man, sitting at an otherwise deserted counter, rhythmically spooning into his mouth what Ferrine imagined was his supper, from a mound of something on a plate that looked like dumplings and chopped beef hunks and kidney beans, holding in his other hand a petrified slab of cornbread dripping with butter.

Ferrine, coming up behind him, said, "You're under arrest. Eating a meal like that without a doctor's prescription."

Slowly, Sheriff Anders turned and grinned.

It always made them, each of them, feel good just to be together.

"I see you finally got smart and threw away your badge," said Anders. "What you doing these days? Drummerin' tea and extracts?"

"I haven't thrown it way," said Ferrine. "I sent it to Chicago to get it gold plated and set with rubies and emeralds."

"What brings you sneaking into Farley at this hour?"

Ferrine took a seat beside his friend. A counterman appeared and Ferrine said, "Pie? Coffee."

The counterman left. Ferrine showed Anders the telegram.

Anders read it swiftly, and handed it back.

"I didn't send it," he said.

"I know that now."

Anders seemed to meditate. He was a real old-timer, long-haired. He was invariably garbed in a blue cotton shirt, a paint pony hide vest, blue twill trousers, and serviceable calfskin boots.

The counterman appeared with a piece of dried apple pie and a mug of coffee, and again vanished.

Ferrine stared at the pie.

"That's pie," said Anders.

"I can tell by the size and shape," said Ferrine.

"Farley style," said Anders. "Nice and ugly."

"I'm going to eat it," said Ferrine. "Yes sir, I'm going to eat it."

"Go right ahead. It's your property. You paid for it."

"I'm going to eat it just to watch Annie's face when I tell her about it. I bet she never heard of such a thing. Pie made out of old shoe-tongues."

He took a bite.

Sheriff Anders asked, "Did this Holt Wallace, whoever he is, show up?"

"A man carrying a stockman's association membership card, with the name T. L. Cloud, showed up."

"Cloud!" exclaimed Sheriff Anders. "Of all people, Cloud. What happened?"

"He drew and I shot and killed him."

"*Drew?*" said Anders. "I've knowed T. L. Cloud for nigh twenty year and never seen him with a gun. I wouldn't have guessed he'd have even drawed on a Apache."

"Well, he sure as hell drew on me."

"I wonder why . . ."

"Because he was set up to do it," said Ferrine. "The same person who sent that fake telegram worked on *him*, too. Told him watch out for strangers when you get there, they're after you, or some such story. Spooked him good and proper."

"I'll have to carry the sad news to his wife immediate, poor lady," said Anders. "But first we'll just drop by the depot."

They left the eatery, made their way to the town's big business section, and strolled along the uneven

10

boardwalk. Farley was much larger than S-burg. The shops, at this pre-dawn hour, were dark, the saloons glared and blared, and the passersby were few. Sheriff Anders said, "This is the first time I ever heard of a sheriff being used as a hired gun."

"Hired and didn't get paid anything," said Ferrine dryly.

"And you aim to collect?"

"In some way or other," said Ferrine coldly. "I can tell you one thing. I don't aim to shake my finger under someone's nose and give them a scolding."

The little station, when they came through its front door, was indistinct in half-light, its single lamp with wick turned low giving off more greasy smoke than illumination. There were two double benches, like pews set back to back, for passengers, and the pine floor had been oiled with something, probably engine oil. The benches were empty and there was no one behind the counter. Sheriff Anders, raising his voice, called, "Jode!"

A man appeared from behind a baize curtain at the far rear, and stood behind the counter facing them, his hands splayed down on the countertop. He was lanky and shrewd looking, and wore a blue and white polka dot nightgown. He also wore an eyeshade. *I wonder if he sleeps in that eyeshade*, Ferrine thought. *Always ready for business.* "Howdy, Sheriff," he said brightly and gallantly. "At your service."

Anders said, "Jode, this is Sheriff Ferrine, from over at S-burg. We want to know who got you to send a telegram you sent. Show it to him, Bill."

11

Ferrine handed over the telegram.

Jode read it, and read it again. He handed it back.

"It wasn't sent from here," he declared.

"It had to be," said Anders. "It says it was."

"That means nothing," said Jode. "And all these serial numbers and all. They mean nothing either. I'd say they was just made up."

Anders and Ferrine looked at each other blankly.

Jode said, "I live here. I'm never beyond the sound of my key. If it was a joke, I'd call it a mighty poor joke."

"It wasn't a joke," said Anders. "Well, I'm sorry we woke you. Thanks."

Still Ferrine delayed. Finally, he said, "It had to be sent over a telegraph wire. That means some station had to send it. Friend, do you think you could do this? Could you send out an inquiry, say to every station a couple of hundred miles up and down the line, and ask if any of them sent it?"

"Of course," said Jode. "But it'll cost a little money. Not much, but some. We better get straight who is going to pay for it, Stantonsburg or Farley?"

"Farley," said Ferrine.

"Snakesburg," said Anders.

"Why don't you cut high card for it?" said Jode helpfully.

"With him?" said Anders scornfully. "No, please. We'll just split the cost."

They left.

Outside, the sky was beginning to show a faint pearl tint in the east. Sheriff Anders said, "I hate to tell you, Bill, but a idea just come to me."

12

Sourly, Ferrine said, "What?"

"That we'll never know who sent it. It didn't have to be sent from no station. It could have been sent from out on the prairie, or out on the desert, wherever the wire runs. Anybody could have just cut in with a homemade handset and sent; a child could have put a workable instrument together, and even done the cuttin' in. In the Big War, when Morgan raided up into Ohio, that was one of the things he did, tapped into telegraph lines and throwed the Yankees into a mix-up by sendin' false messages. Anyone that can tell a dot from a dash can learn Morse."

They crossed the tracks, entered the unpainted clapboard face of a building — through a small door set in a big door — and Ferrine found himself in a livery stable.

Anders said, "I'm goin' out and notify Miss' Sophy about her husband's death. It's about ten miles out. What you want to do?"

"I'm coming along."

"I don't look forward to it."

"Where should I rent a good horse?"

"Right here. Where I keep mine. She lives out near the Mazatzals. Ever been out that way?"

"No."

"Well, well."

Miles of their trip were already behind them when the dawn sun came up, and it came up slowly, molten and golden and almost unbearably hot. Arizona, Ferrine had been told, meant arid belt, and that was it, either

13

arid or semi-arid. Of course, there were areas of lush grass, but it was sure as hell the dry you thought of, and remembered. When the sun hit them, they were in semi-arid country, not out-and-out desert, but close enough.

As soon as there was light enough to see at all, they saw the Mazatzals ahead of them, in the distance. The range itself, a scorching powder-blue in the sun's fire, lay north and south, like a barrier beyond which existed nothing but emptiness.

"Do we cross 'em?" asked Ferrine.

"No," said Anders. "Our place is on hither side. In fact we're almost there."

The ground they rode over, and to either side of them, was paper-thin, and blotched with rocky rubble and mesquite and stinkweed. Occasionally, they passed the giant candelabrum of a parched cactus. There were no cattle. The only movement was the hypnotic weaving of a distant buzzard.

Then, as the mountains loomed closer, the country changed suddenly and without warning and they were in rich buffalo grass and there were cows. "Fresh water from the high country," the Farley sheriff explained.

The ranch house, when they came to it, was sequestered in a maze of low, terraced mesas, in a little patch of green flatland, verdant and fertile in surrounding pasturage. It was a modest structure, no porch (porches, even in the back country, Ferrine knew, were marks of prestige), and rose two stories and stark in weathered gray planking before a barn and outbuildings of exactly the same drab tone and

14

character. A corral with a few pretty good horses in it indicated that it was a working outfit, although a small one. A woman sat on an upended nailkeg, in the sunlight, by the open front door.

She was maybe thirty years old, square-jawed, slit-eyed, and dressed in voluminous navy blue. She was shucking roasting ears, and was barefooted. "Daughter?" asked Ferrine as they approached.

"Wife," said Anders.

"Old husband, young wife," said Ferrine.

"Your words, not mine," said Anders. They swung from their saddles and hitched at a rack.

"Good day, Miss' Sophy," said Anders soberly. "This-here is Sheriff Ferrine of S-burg. I sure hate a duty like this, but I got bad news. Your husband's been kilt."

She seemed not to hear. Meticulously, she finished husking the ear in her hands; delicately, she stroked the kernels.

Steadily, she said, "You mean really dead?"

"Yes ma'am," said Anders.

"How did it happen?" Her voice sounded completely detached.

At first Ferrine thought she didn't understand, then he knew she did, and he felt a chill.

"Sheriff Ferrine here shot him," said Anders.

Never once raising her eyes, she said, "And he came along while you told me."

"He wouldn't have it no other way," said Anders. He handed the girl the telegram. "He thought I sent that, but I didn't. We don't know who sent it."

She read it and handed it back. "Because of the yellow waterproof."

"Yes," said Anders. "Partly."

"And because of the horse-blanket pin."

"That, too," said Anders.

"And because he drew on me when I hailed him," said Ferrine.

"He wouldn't have drawn on you," she said expressionlessly. "He hated guns. He wouldn't have even known how."

Ferrine said, "Well, he did, ma'am. And he was set to kill me. I could see it in his eyes. Wild."

"I'd have did the same," said Anders. "With such a telegram in my pocket."

"The telegram in his pocket," she said. "There was no telegram in his pocket then, of course. He got the stationmaster, probably a friend of his, to write it out afterward." Now looking full at Ferrine, burning him with the intensity of her irises, she asked, "Why? You just kill, is that it? You pin on a star and go around killing?"

Ferrine didn't answer.

"I didn't love him," she said abruptly, and they knew she meant it.

"Don't talk that way, ma'am!" exclaimed Anders.

"I didn't love him, but I was his wife."

"I understand, Miss' Sophy," said Anders, perspiring. "We'd better be getting on, Bill."

"My people came from the Missouri hills," she said. "One thing I learned at my grandmother's knee was to settle accounts. If you owed the crossroads' store seven

16

cents for two needles and a spool of thread, you didn't sleep until you settled the account."

"Let's go, Bill," said Anders.

She said, "Maybe it wasn't only my husband you killed, Sheriff Ferrine, maybe you killed yourself, too."

They mounted, and rode away.

It was just before dusk — the dusty town was stifling from the burn of the low sun — when they got back to Farley and stabled their horses. Ferrine, who had gotten very little sleep on the caboose, was tired and he knew that Anders, who had been up all night and gotten none at all, must be worse. They went to a place called *Louella's Café*, had potatoes hashed up with hickory nut-sized chunks of onion, and a platter of little fried steaks, and came out feeling better.

"Where now?" asked Anders.

"Home, I guess."

"Ready to go? Satisfied?"

"I'm worse off than when I got here," said Ferrine. "Then I just had trouble. Now I'm going to get myself shot by a barefooted woman."

"Why don't you spend the night here?" asked Sheriff Anders. "I got a broke down sofa in my office."

Ferrine considered.

"We ought to talk this over some more," said Anders.

"Maybe we better at that," said Ferrine. "But I won't pull your sofa out from under you. I'll put up at a hotel or rooming house somewhere. You're a good friend, Burt." He watched Anders leave.

Down three timbered steps from the boardwalk, in the center of the street, was the island with the station and its platform. A little girl, on her hunkers on the platform, seemed to be trying to load a shotgun laid out on the planks before her. Ferrine walked over. She was completely absorbed in her project.

She was trying to load it with little brass screws and horseshoe nails.

Ferrine said, "That's a pretty mean load."

"I want it to be," she said.

"For anybody in particular?" he asked.

"For anybody that strikes my fancy," she said. "I'm short-tempered."

He watched her in silence.

She seemed to enjoy his presence.

He saw that someone, an adult certainly, had jammed the lock by hammering it so that the gun was perfectly harmless.

"It's for people," she explained. "I don't like people."

"What's your name?" he asked.

She was about eleven, freckled, tight-mouthed. She wore a plaid calico dress, and black cotton stockings sagged on her thin reedlike legs. If he'd ever looked at a tomboy, he was looking at one now, Ferrine decided.

She said, "Do you have a chew of tobacco on you?"

Ferrine shook his head.

"My name's Henry," she said.

"Then whoever named you was blind," said Ferrine. "You look mighty like a little girl to me."

"I ain't reached man's estate as yet."

"Live around here?" asked Ferrine.

"You're standing in my front yard," she said. "My pa's Jode, the man that owns that little shanty behind you."

"You mean the stationmaster?"

"And will be until he retires. Then, o' course, I'll take over."

Conversationally, Ferrine said, "I wouldn't want to be a stationmaster. A man has to cut his own hair."

"What do you mean?" she said, surprised and confused. "They go to the barbershop like anyone else."

"Your father kind of gave me the idea he was handcuffed to his office, twenty-four hours a day."

"That's foolish. He's in and out, like anyone else. He goes to the Court Square Tonsorial Parlor for *his* barbering."

"Who holds down the place when he's gone?"

"I do."

"I mean like the telegraph."

"I do. There's nothing to it."

Ferrine looked slightly skeptical. "You mean you can receive?"

"Easy."

"And send?"

"Easy."

Hardly had she spoken than she looked scared.

"Henry," said Ferrine gently, "I got you."

He showed her his badge. "I'm the man you sent it to. Better tell me all about it."

"You did that pretty slick," she said in admiration.

"Let's have it. Tell me about it."

"Pa was out buying a center-cut slice of ham for our supper," she said hesitantly.

"Go on."

"I was behind the counter at the desk and this man came in with a piece of wrapping paper with this message on it and asked me to send it, and I did."

"Did he pay you?"

"He gave me a handful of grocery store chocolate drops. He said it was a joke."

"Can you describe the man?"

"I can do better than that. I can tell you who he was. It was Texas Slim."

Ferrine looked encouraging.

The child said, "You know, the hobo, the handyman at Trenchard's store over there." She pointed.

"Thanks," said Ferrine.

"There ain't no harm in us being sensible about this," she said. "I won't tell nobody about this if you don't."

"Good enough," said Ferrine. "You have my word no one will get it out of me."

He left the platform and headed back toward Main Street.

CHAPTER
THREE

Trenchard's store was on a corner, two stories of brown painted, spongy-looking poplar planking. Its show window displayed guns, bonnets, an open barrel of ribbon hard-candy, and a rosette of cheap spurs hanging on a logchain from a meat hook. By the door, there was a bench, empty.

Ferrine entered.

He found himself in a labyrinth of tables and aisles, merchandise of every variety everywhere. The place was cavernously deserted now for it was suppertime, but soon families, food in their stomachs, would be back on Main Street again, socializing, promenading, shopping. The owner was fussing around, lighting lamps and adjusting their tin reflectors. He was dressed in soft expensive tan wool, a tall calm man, glinting gold at cuff links, collar button, and watchfob. His sparse hair was combed back over a shiny blotched skull. Ferrine joined him.

"Mr. Trenchard?" he asked.

The man nodded.

"Sizable store," said Ferrine.

"The largest in town, I think," said Trenchard modestly, "How can I serve you?"

Some men showed you everything they were on the surface; here, Ferrine felt, was one with much in reserve.

"I'm looking for a man, a hobo, known as Texas Slim," said Ferrine. "Folks around town say I can find him here."

"Yesterday but not today," said Trenchard regretfully.

"Let's have that again," said Ferrine.

"He was my man of all work," said Trenchard. "He also drove my delivery dray around town. He spent all his spare time on that bench outside by the door. Everybody knew him and liked him. The bench is empty now, you see."

"I see."

"This morning, he came in, showed me twenty dollars — which I certainly didn't give him — and quit."

"Where is he now?"

"Who knows?" said Trenchard. "Long gone. A drifter."

"Where do you think he got that twenty dollars?"

"He could have got it anywhere. He knew everybody in town. Some say he peddled untaxed, unlicensed whisky from the bench and off of my dray, but I don't believe it. I'd say he won it rolling dice at the livery stable. Who are you, by the way, and why do you want him?"

Ferrine said, "I'm his brother from New Mexico. He got mad at the breakfast table one morning and walked away from his pancakes and we haven't seen him since.

22

Ma is lonesome for him and I'm trying to trace him down and talk him into coming back."

"That's a pretty sad story," said Trenchard. "And not too different from my own."

Something about this man's poise disturbed Ferrine; he said, "We want him to stop this roaming and come home. We've just annexed Mr. Johnson's place — he's our near-neighbor — and we need him bad."

"Well, you almost got him," said Trenchard tranquilly. "So near and yet so far. Better luck next time. How did you ever happen to come here, to Farley?"

"One thing led to another," Ferrine said vaguely.

Suddenly Trenchard laughed. He'd been having a wonderful time. He said, "I don't know where your man is, and I wouldn't tell you if I did. I don't meddle around with the law, one way or other. And this is outside your jurisdiction, Sheriff Ferrine."

"You know me?" asked Ferrine.

"I used to live in S-burg," said Trenchard.

Ferrine walked from the store, out into the town.

Shops were lighted now, and people were gathering on the walks, chatting, laughing, enjoying the cool of the evening. He went in search of a bed. Any kind of a bed, anywhere.

The place he found was called Aunt Mary's, a rooming house, and the Aunt Mary that took his dollar and showed him up the stairs was an old man, unshaven, filthy, and so drunk he could hardly make it up the ladder-steep steps. The room was first cousin to a broom closet. The bed was an old canvas cot, but he hit it fully clothed, minus only his boots, and slept as though he had been pole-axed. He awoke about seven-thirty, rested but starving, had a thick steak with eggs on it at a railroad café that he had noticed around the corner, and headed for the courthouse. In the brash stark gold of the early morning, the town looked dead, hollow, menacing. Towns like Farley weren't daylight towns.

Sheriff Anders was in his office at the courthouse, behind his desk, deep in the exhausting and loathsome part of his job, the paperwork. He was a man, Ferrine had long discovered, who could go on forever; he couldn't have had more than a few hours sleep, but he looked completely refreshed and ready to rip into another twenty-four hours.

He smiled, and Ferrine sat down.

"Learn anything?" asked Anders.

"I don't know," said Ferrine, protecting Henry and her illegal telegram.

"When are you going back to S-burg?"

"On the next eastbound, I guess," said Ferrine.

"There's one at nine-twelve," said Anders.

"That'll be fine," said Ferrine.

"You're holding back something on me," said Anders shrewdly.

"Nothing important," said Ferrine. "How long were Cloud and his wife married?"

"They weren't married. They just lived together."

Ferrine looked amazed. "I heard her say she was his wife. That was the very word she used, wife."

"Preachers are scarce in that back country," said Anders. "And they never seemed to get around to it or something when they come to Farley. They jumped over the broomstick."

"Well, then, that's that," said Ferrine. "Don't laugh, but once I had the spooky idea maybe she'd set him up for death herself."

Anders didn't laugh. He said, "Why would she?"

"To inherit, I thought, maybe. I see now she wouldn't inherit."

"She'll inherit. Whatever there is. You seen it yourself, it can't be much."

"I don't follow you."

"A similar case come up here some time back. I disremember all the ins and outs of it, but here is the situation. In the eyes of the law, a true common-law wife is a wife, a legal wife. If they live together for such and such a length of time, and she uses his name openly, when he shuffles off she gets about the same portion of his estate as a bona fide properly sanctified and license-stapled widow."

"They outwit you coming and going, don't they?" said Ferrine.

"Anything else, Bill?"

"I stopped in Trenchard's store. He didn't much like me, and I didn't much like him. What about him? He says he once lived in Stantonsburg, but naturally I don't recall him, with a town of that size."

"Naturally, with a town of that size. Well, Tom Trenchard's okay, if you don't expect him to act decent like other people. That's the way you make a million dollars, you know, Bill."

"No, I didn't know. But I often wondered. I hope he stays up here in Farley." Ferrine got up.

Sheriff Anders said, "It could be nobody ever finishes this one, Bill."

Ferrine shook his head noncommittally.

They didn't shake hands. They knew and liked each other too well for fripperies. Ferrine left.

The eastbound slammed into the Stantonsburg station a little after noon, and Ferrine got down. Almost before his feet were on the platform, its pistons were churning again and it was off. He was home again, back at the one place in the world he knew inside and out, up and down, but he felt no happiness at being here, only distress and frustration and anger.

He was standing in the fiery sun, brooding, just where the train had deposited him, when the stationmaster came out of the depot — the same man who had started it all with that fake wanted-dead-or-alive-don't-take-any-chances-with-this-man message — and said cheerily, "Welcome home, Bill. Here's another wire come in for you about a hour ago."

Ferrine took the paper and read it.

It said: *Keeping your mouth shut about me appreciated one good turn deserves another so here goes (stop) papa out at moment sampling suds (stop) he found message on counter weighted down with five dollar goldpiece so nacherally got it off (stop) never did see sender (stop) neither him nor me couldn't later make out scribbled signature (stop) Sunset Joe Grenada Theba Arizona get them three friends of yours from Gila Bend and get here to me in Farley County quickly for personal job eight hundred apiece guaranteed (stop) this sounds like sheriff business so am passing it on to my favorite sheriff (stop) this sounds gun thrower to me and them that hides at Gila Bend is said to be quicker and meaner than scorpions swak (signed) Henry.*

"I don't get that swak," said the stationmaster. "I queried this Henry on it, but he wouldn't change it."

Wonderful little Henry, Ferrine thought. With her pipe-stem legs and chewing tobacco and baggy black cotton stockings.

Ferrine shook his head.

He wondered what Annie had had for noonday dinner, and if there was any left.

He started home to see.

It turned out to be one of his favorite meals, vegetable soup so thick you could almost slice it with a knife, which she reheated for him, and leftover mush, medium thin and fried crisp, which he always liked to eat in his hand like bread, and she served it cold because he enjoyed it that way.

As he ate, she studied him. She said, "No bloody holes, no bruises, apparently no broken bones. I see they returned you undamaged and as received. Tell me all about it. What did you do there?"

"Got shouting happy drunk," Ferrine said. "Lost our home at poker, and won it back at faro. Helled around, reveled, orgied. Met some nice girls. Misspent my life in just about every wonderful way you can think of."

She grinned. "You don't fool me, Bill. You had bad luck, didn't you?"

"I didn't have any luck at all, good or bad."

"Well, you've got to remember that happens sometimes."

"If you say so."

"And you've no idea who sent that message?"

"It could have been Mrs. Cloud, the man's common-law wife, but I doubt if anyone will ever be able to prove it. You ought to see her, Annie, and talk to her about three minutes."

"I don't want to. So you'd say it's finished?"

"I can't see any other answer. Finished."

"Thank God," she said.

"Thank God for what? I killed an innocent man."

"I didn't like this one," she said. "I wish you'd stick to rustlers and bank robbers."

"Or better yet," he agreed, "just advising people about things. Storekeepers to keep their back doors locked, little boys not to play with matches, old maids not to take up with strange men. Those are our duties, too. And I've been neglecting them."

It was about ten minutes later when Bill Junior came in from town with the second telegram. It said: *Thanks to your help think have got our little problem on way to settlement and will inform you personally in day or two — Albertus.*

"Who is this Albertus?" asked Annie.

"Burt. Burt Anders," said Ferrine. "That's his real name. I'm one of about a half dozen that knows it. He wants me to know *this* telegram from him is genuine."

"Then it isn't all finished," she said fearfully.

"I'd say yes," said Ferrine. "As smart as Burt Anders is, and he's smart, I doubt if he can out-smart our Mrs. Sophy Cloud. I'd bet my bottom dollar that right this minute he's thinking exactly what she wants him to."

All along, he had been mighty careful not to mention to Annie anything about any Sunset Joe Grenada.

A couple of weeks went by, nothing of major importance in the law enforcement department happened at Stantonsburg, and there was no further word from Farley. It was just the millwheel routine of work, everything from bastardy complaints out in the county to fence line squabbles; he made a point of pacifying fence line trouble himself, personally, because fence line trouble went into blood feuds, easy, and anything could come out of a blood feud.

One morning, he paused at the blacksmith shop in passing to watch the smith's helper, an itinerant worker, forge and temper, in fancy curlicues, some wrought iron work for the bank. These helpers, temporary and down at the heels, appeared suddenly and vanished just as suddenly — and were always magical at their trade, always much better, in fact, than their employers. They were never outlaws, always affable, and their sole enemy was popskull rotgut. They talked a lot, but shrewdly said nothing, and it was a waste of time, Ferrine had long ago discovered, to try to get any local information from them. Ferrine was watching the fellow's delicate anvilwork, when he felt a touch on his shoulder and turned.

The man behind him was unknown to him, sleek, smug, well-fed looking, overbearing in his manner. He was a townsman from somewhere, Ferrine decided; townsman dressed in mixed tweed clothing and with a cable-type watchchain about the size of a well-rope. His eyes were like little slivers of limestone, and his jowl slabs were drooping and flabby.

He said, "Sheriff Ferrine?"

Ferrine said yes.

"Let's find someplace to talk," said the man. "Someplace private. I've got something to tell you."

Ferrine walked out of the shop with him, down the street, to a sidewalk bench before the seven foot plank fence of a hideyard. They sat down.

"I'm Sheriff Lumsden, Sheriff," the man said.

"Glad to know you," said Ferrine, not feeling comfortable about all this hocus-pocus. "Where from?"

"Farley," said the man.

"Farley where?" asked Ferrine.

"Farley, Arizona," said the man. "The county next to yours, the town just up the railroad track. Don't tell me you've never heard of us." He smiled sarcastically. "I know better."

A blackness came and went before Ferrine's eyes, and a numbness needled his forearms and upturned hands. Finally, he said. "Has Farley got two sheriffs now? It's Burt Anders I know."

30

"Burt Anders has had an unfortunate decease," said the man. "I'm filling his unexpired term."

"What do you mean?"

"He had a gunfight with four out-of-towners, drifters, and came out loser."

Bleakly, Ferrine said, "How many of the drifters came out loser?"

"None. Sheriff Anders was outclassed. Those that saw it, said they were veteran gunhands."

"Where did it take place?"

"In the court square. They were waiting for him. In the open. Yesterday."

"Where are they now?"

"Who knows? Gone."

Futilely, desperately, hoping for any kind of a way to make it untrue, Ferrine said, "Who appointed you to take his place?"

"The County Commissioners," said Lumsden. He produced identification documents that couldn't be doubted.

Ferrine read them twice and handed them back. Stunned, he said, "You don't look like a sheriff exactly, what were you before?"

"Chairman of the County Commissioners," said Sheriff Lumsden.

CHAPTER
FOUR

Ferrine said, "But why the trip to Stantonsburg? What do you want with me."

"I thought we'd best have a little talk together and get this thing straight right from the very beginning. I have the franchise on Farley County, you have the franchise on Stanton County. The law says the county line is the borderline between us, and it's the same as an invisible barbwire fence between us. You don't cross it and mess with me, and I don't cross it and mess with you. Right?"

"Some people call it bailiwick," said Ferrine. "Not franchise."

"I used to be a businessman," said Sheriff Lumsden. "And it seems like I can't get rid of business talk. You get the point, though, don't you?"

"I'm not sure. What is the point."

"I don't want you meddling in Farley. Farley is in good hands."

"Did you tell this to all the sheriffs bordering your county?" asked Ferrine.

"No, but I will sooner or later. When the necessity arises."

Ferrine stared at him coldly and decided he had the face of a caterpillar under a reading glass.

He said, "What business were you in, before you were sheriff, before you were commissioner, Mr. Lumsden?"

"I traveled in notions and sundries, pearl buttons, ladies' elastic tape, whalebone corset stays, tatting needles, imitation Irish lace, and the like. It took a real man to handle it. There were a million stock items to remember. And that's the way the Farley sheriff's office is going to be run from now on."

"You mean peddling elastic and corset stays?"

"No, certainly. But you're beginning to get the concept."

"Am I?"

"It costs money to run a sheriff's office, doesn't it?"

"That's what I hear."

"Right. Why can't it be self-supporting? Or better yet, show a profit? A good substantial juicy profit?"

"Others have tried that," said Ferrine.

"I don't mean *that* way," said Lumsden. "I mean all legal and aboveboard. Would you care to hear more on the subject?"

"I sure would," said Ferrine.

"To get back to notions," said Lumsden. "The elastic showed three times the profit percentage the pearl buttons did. The same must be true in a sheriff's office, bigger profits in this, say, than that. I'd say the answer would be in cutting unnecessary and unprofitable expense and in being selective in what you push."

"You mean in what crimes you push?"

33

"No. I mean certain aspects, like fees and serving papers, seem to me more profitable, *per se*, and less time-wasting than long futile treks after stage robbers, say."

"And let the next sheriff down the line look after the stage robber."

"That's what he gets paid for, isn't it?"

"You know something, Mr. Lumsden," said Ferrine. "When this began, I wasn't sure I liked you. I've changed my mind. It's a pleasure just to listen to you. Can I ask you a question? Say I simply have to come to Farley. Will I get charged as a trespasser?"

"Of course not. Alien sheriffs are always welcome, if they come as private citizens. And not disturbers."

"Did you buy yourself a new gun when you were appointed?" asked Ferrine.

"No. But, matter of fact, I did buy myself a complete new outfit of clothes, suit, hat, socks, shoes, and so on. Clothes make the man, as we used to say."

"Well, goodbye, Sheriff Lumsden," said Ferrine, arising. "I've got to be getting along. Tell me, do you ever worry about your predecessor?"

"Sheriff Anders? Death cometh to us all, and passeth all understanding."

"And the four men that killed him are far away and long gone."

"Amen."

That was Monday forenoon. At exactly 1:03a.m. Wednesday, Ferrine was back in Farley, this time with his accordian valise.

He came unannounced. There was no Sheriff Lumsden with, say, a posse of businessmen, waiting on the platform to meet him. Through the depot window, he could see the empty waiting room and the empty space behind the counter, dim in the nightlight: the stationmaster and Henry were abed. He headed for Aunt Mary's rooming house. There was a dry chill to the darkness. He'd left his chief deputy, Keeno Williams, in charge as acting sheriff, saying he wasn't certain how long he'd be gone, and Keeno was entirely competent.

At Aunt Mary's, the same filthy drunken old man took him up the steep stairs and ensconced him in a different, but identical, broom closet. Again, he slept soundly on the sagging canvas cot. He was awake at dawn, and dressed. He could find no washbowl in the room, nor pitcher of water. He put his valise under the cot, left the room, left the house, looked in the backyard for a privy, and found one, of all things, padlocked. He washed his hands and splashed water on his face at a watering trough on Main Street, had two hard boiled eggs, crackers, and a fishbowl of beer at a saloon, being careful not to socialize with the touch-and-go dawn occupants, felt better, and looked up the livery stable he had used before. They remembered him. He rented the same horse he'd had before, the tough little roan he'd liked so well, used the livery stable privy, and left town. He had no traveling supplies if he should need them, but it was too early to buy any, and he'd have to meet that problem later. The pressing urge now was to get going, get this thing started.

He had decided to swing in a big half-circle and come down on the Cloud place from the rear, for no especial reason except that it would be unexpected, and there was always advantage in being unexpected.

For a while he followed the same route he and Anders had taken, then he veered left. The sun came up, and the country was unfamiliar to him, but he was a veteran at tracking from the saddle, which had given him an almost intuitive sense of direction; also, if he really needed a guide, there were always the stark Mazatzals in the near distance.

As the mountain escarpments, with their sparse cedar and juniper and locust, became clearer through the cloud wisps, the going underfoot became rougher, but the little roan could hold her own. First, Ferrine wove his way through a maze of short low ridges, rocky and razor-topped, unconnected, and divided from each other by cañons and gullies. Occasionally, he saw, scattered close and distant, like a throw of dice, terraced volcanic mesas, harsh and lonesome looking. This was desert, and bad; the question was how far it extended. Deserts were irregular in shape and size, and you never knew.

Again he turned his roan, this time right, then, later, right again. Just before sunset he made his last turn, once more right, and knew he was approaching the Cloud place from the rear, and that it couldn't be too far away. Boulders and stunted greasewood dwindled into sage and bunchgrass, and all at once the land was fertile, and there were fat calves about him.

All this sudden richness, he knew, was due to the nearness of the mountains and the little fresh water mountain streams which crisscrossed the tableland around him. You could tell the presence of the streams long before you reached them from the cottonwoods which always thicketed their banks.

He reached a stream, particularly inviting, decided to take a drink, and dismounted.

He was in sort of a pocket enclosed by cottonwoods and their thick wild undergrowth. There was a jumble of pocked and weathered rocks, round, some the size of his fist, some eight or ten feet high. The stream, narrow, crystal, swift moving, circled the base of the largest boulder, flattened itself a little farther down in a puddled bog of marsh, regathered and continued out of sight. He lowered himself, knelt at the base of the boulder, and drank from cupped hands. He'd made the dipping motion twice, when a calm voice said, "Tastes good, eh?"

Ferrine looked up. A grizzled old cowman was across the stream from him, sitting tranquilly on his heels, knees spread in worn batwing chaps. He wore his gun high on his hip, non-belligerent, self-protecting only, old-time cowboy style, and idly chewed a grass stem.

"Howdy," said the old man genially. "How do you feel? Up to now?"

"What do you mean, up to now?" said Ferrine, alert, but too late.

He had scrambled half upright from his knees and his weapon had cleared leather when someone behind him hit him with the side of a gun that felt as heavy as a sledge, loose held in the palm, loose swung, just over the ear with a crash that knocked him half silly.

He went somehow disconnected in his bone joints, slewed to the earth, lay there, then fought his way upright to his feet and balance.

He must have been out when he was on the ground because now there were two men in sight, the other having crossed the stream, each of them standing patiently by a horse, leaning against a saddle, watching him and waiting. On the horn of one of their saddles hung his gun and buckled gunbelt.

The other, the one that had hit him, was a boy about sixteen, all working cowhand and no nonsense. He had a flat-crowned worn hat, straight straw-colored hair, and had a small kerchief about his throat above his Adam's apple, knotted at the side. He wore his gun like the older man, high, non-gunfighter style. They looked like what they were, Ferrine was certain, damned good honest laboring men.

The old man said, "Hungry?"

"No," said Ferrine, who hadn't eaten anything since his dawn breakfast of two eggs and beer. "And I wouldn't take anything off you two sons of bitches if I was."

"The way you come, you must have come across the desert strip," said the old man. "We looked into your saddlebags. No food nor sign o' food. You rode hungry."

"Who are you?" asked Ferrine. Then, trying to really insult them, his head splitting, he asked, "Gun crazy sheepmen?"

"We ain't gun crazy and we ain't sheepmen," said the boy, bridling. "And watch your mouth, trespasser, or I'll hit you again."

"I wish to hell I could coax you into trying it," said Ferrine.

The old man intervened. "Tolliver," he said to the boy. "On rare occasions I've seen men like this'un before. I don't believe I'd meddle with him, armed or unarmed, if I was you. They's a kind of human you don't know nothing about, son, and what have you done but caught yourself one? I'd start being mannerly before he has you eatin' your own gunsight, even if you have got him so helpless lookin'."

"I don't take that as a compliment," said Ferrine.

"It wasn't meant as a compliment," said the old man. "It was just a word o' advice to a youngster who ain't yet had the advantages of the ways o' the world."

"He don't scare me," said the boy grudgingly.

"And the circle-saw don't scare the log," said the old man. "Let's get back to Miss' Sophy and her breaded pork chops." To Ferrine, he said, "Come along."

As they rode along, Ferrine asked the old man, "Do you treat all your visitors this way?"

"Strangers, yes," said the old man. "Miss' Sophy wantin' it that way for the time bein', her so alone and all."

He came into the Cloud place from the rear, all right, as he had planned, but through the back door

39

into the kitchen, half walking, half supported, and minus his gun, which hung in its holster from its belt, looped over the shoulder of a towheaded youngster beside him.

They deposited him on a chair by the table; he slumped forward a moment on the oilcloth of the tabletop, head enfolded in his arms, and then straightened. His eyes were focusing properly now, and his mind seemed reasonably clear. First he inspected the three around the edge of the table, watching him, the boy who had hit him, the old man, and Mrs. Cloud, stocky and strong, Cherokee faced, steady eyed. Somewhere along the line, while he was still groggy, darkness had fallen. A barn lantern had been lit and placed before him so they could see him better, and the room, frugal and bare, was goldenrod yellow and layered with greasy kerosene smoke. Mrs. Cloud said, "There's blood on his ear. Who hit him and where did you find him?"

The old man said, "Tolliver hit him. We found him back in the Pine Finger range, by the creek there. You said no trespassers, bring 'em in, so that's what we done."

To Ferrine, Mrs. Cloud said, in explanation, not apology, "Tolliver got a horse ambushed out from under him two days ago."

"Who are they?" asked Ferrine.

"They're my two hands. The elderly gentleman, Mr. Layton, is the best cowman north of the border, the younger one is Tolliver. I'd match the pair of them against a six man crew." To Tolliver, she said, "You'll never guess what you fetched in. A sheriff."

"And a gunfighter, too," said Mr. Layton. "If I can trust sixty-odd years of instinct."

The boy's face went congested red, then bloodless white.

Numbly, he said, "Anybody can make a mistake."

"That ain't too wise a saying," said the oldster. "Give him back his gun."

"He'll shoot me," said the boy.

"Will you?" asked Layton.

"How do I know?" said Ferrine gravely. "We'll just have to wait and see."

The boy handed him his gunbelt. Ferrine buckled it on. The boy stood popeyed, helpless.

Mr. Layton said, "Now put some bacon and pones in his saddlebag. He'll have to have something when he leaves us." The boy got the articles together and left the room.

Mrs. Cloud said, "How about some nice marrow broth and cornbread right now?"

"If you say so," said Ferrine. She brought him a steaming savory bowl and bread. "Last time I saw you, you hated me, now you love me," he said.

"I wouldn't go that far," she said. "But it was the ambush, and the receipt. Now I believe you, now I know you were innocent."

"What about the ambush?" asked Ferrine. "I'd dearly like to know about that."

"Tolliver was coming back from riding fence. The bushwhacker missed him, got his mount instead, and hightailed. Tolliver never laid eyes on him. None of the three of us got any idea who or why."

"What about the receipt?" asked Ferrine. "What do you mean by that?"

She went into the house proper and returned with a small square of paper. "I found this with some other documents in my husband's strongbox," she said. She laid it before him. It said:

RECEIVED OF *T. L. Cloud*
Five Hundred & Eighty Dollars & no cents
                    (signed)
                    Luke Opperson
                    March 2, 1897

"Who is Luke Opperson?" asked Ferrine.

"I haven't the slightest idea. I never heard of him," declared Mrs. Cloud.

"You think this Opperson was squeezing him?" asked Ferrine.

"No one ever squeezed my husband," she said. "If anything, it was always the other way around. I think, and am sure, that my husband bought something from him last year. Something he didn't mention to me. Something I don't know about."

"Was that like your husband, to have secrets from you?"

"It sure was. Especially about money."

"What do you think he bought?"

"Cows," she said firmly. "That was the only thing on earth he would have spent that much money on."

"Did new cows come in here about then?"

She shook her head. "Not then or later."

"Then it doesn't make sense."

"It would if you knew my husband. You know what I think? I think he had another ranch under another name someplace else. And if one, why not two? Or more?"

"And he really died a rich man?" said Ferrine.

"Why not? Under different names, in different places."

Ferrine, disturbed, said, "Do you think you could be building up a lot on very little?"

"Wait," she said. Once more she left the room. This time she returned with an envelope which she handed him. "That's the envelope it came in," she said, turning it over so *he could read the address: Mr. T. L. Cloud, c/o Trenchard's Store, Farley, Arizona.* There was no return address. There was a postmark, though: *Harrington.*

"What's wrong with that?" asked Ferrine, not liking it.

"Why Trenchard's, clear into Farley?" she said. "We get our mail at Charlie Folansbee's, a little ranch house grocery store post office, about two miles behind us, back in the foothills."

Ferrine got unsteadily to his feet. "I'll be getting along. Thanks for the broth."

"Oh, no you don't," she said. "If my boys beat you up, the least I can do is sleep you somewhere."

"I'll sleep on the ground," said Ferrine. "It's my favorite bed."

"Suit yourself," she said. "You're a growed man."

Ferrine asked, "Did you ever hear of a Sunset Joe Grenada?"

"No."

"Or of an Arizona town called Theba?"

"I think so. Up in the northern part of the territory." It was south.

"Help you to the door?" asked Mr. Layton solicitously, not moving. Ferrine shook his head.

CHAPTER
FIVE

The show window at Trenchard's store was the same as before — dismal; only a few dead flies had been added. Ferrine had spent the night on the ground, as he had told Mr. Layton he would, had reached Farley, stabled his mare and settled for her use, and here it was, night again, about nine. After a quick but generous meal at the railroad restaurant, enough to satisfy the strictures of his past two days, he wandered down Main Street, taking it easy, a toothpick in the corner of his lips, feeling good from the food, feeling that maybe now he was really getting someplace. This was the hour when sociability among the harmless level of citizens was at its highest; he pleasured in this, too, the laughter and gay hoots everywhere about him. It would be an hour before the shops began to close, and another before the streets emptied and the other world came out and began to take over. Inside the store, Ferrine stood a moment by the doorjamb, and looked.

When he left this place, he could have the answer to nothing, or he could have the answer to everything. People, farmers, ranchers, townsmen, were buying and inspecting just about everything: ribbons, brass-toed children's shoes, drawstring drawers, rock powder for stump blasting, yeast-bricks for delicious bread, or to put a potency in your cider that would leave you cross-eyed. There was no sight of Mr. Trenchard himself.

Then, quietly, a voice at Ferrine's side said, "Accept my condolence, Sheriff Ferrine."

It was Trenchard. Ferrine said shortly, "Why?"

"On the death of your friend, Burt Anders."

Deeply moved at the memory, at having a picture of the slaughter come before his eyes, Ferrine said, "Thank you, Mr. Trenchard. You're right. He was a friend."

He glanced at Trenchard, tall, expensive in his soft tan wool, sparse haired — and calm. Too calm to be sentimental. And he suddenly wondered if he was being manipulated. If the man was deliberately stirring him emotionally, in that way gaining ascendency in the conversation, placing himself in a position to guide it.

"I was just out to visit Mrs. T. L. Cloud," said Ferrine.

Trenchard looked surprised. "You were? I've heard the story since I last talked with you. I understand it was you that got fancy free with that handgun of yours and killed her perfectly harmless husband. What did she say?"

"She said her husband received secret mail here, in care of your store."

"It could be," said Trenchard. "But I wouldn't call it secret. It's just a little convenience I offer to quite a few of my back-country customers."

"Name two others. Name one other."

"Of course not. Mail delivery is confidential."

"For the life of me," said Ferrine, "I can't see how it's much of a service, if any. The post office itself is only two blocks from here."

"When they ask me, I do it," said Trenchard. "That's all. Different people do different things different ways. My job is to keep everybody happy. That's why Trenchard's is one of —"

"The most profitable store in town," said Ferrine. "You've already told me that. Do you remember how many letters Mr. Cloud got this way? A lot? A few?"

"I'd say a few. Maybe one at six months' intervals. But I wouldn't want to swear to it."

"From Stantonsburg, St. Louis, where? Can you recall?"

"It so happens I *can* recall. From Harrington. All of them."

"How come it sticks in your mind? Did he talk them over with you?"

"No. I remember because they always made him mad when he got them."

Harrington was a little cowtown down the track, about halfway between Farley and S-burg.

"I wonder why they made him mad," said Ferrine. "The one I saw was just a receipt. A receipt by a man named Opperson. Do you know a man named Luke Opperson?"

Trenchard said, "By sight. I've met him a couple of times. But I certainly know who he is!"

"Don't tell me he's a famous Harrington outlaw, or something like that, and I haven't heard of him," said Ferrine.

"Just the opposite," said Trenchard stiffly. "In fact, he's a very respectable and affluent cattleman. Not only cows, a money maker in a good many fields. Mortgage dealer, land dealer, about anything that turns a penny. He's called the Big Man of Harrington."

"He is? Who calls him that?"

"He calls himself that, I believe. You know, of course, that I'm going to have to report this visit of yours here to our new sheriff, Sheriff Lumsden?"

"Go right ahead. I'm going to drop in on him myself in a little bit. By the way, how do you like him?"

"We shopkeepers think he's our kind of man. Decent, sound, cautious. Someone said he's going to pass a law, no horse racing on Sunday."

"Do you have horse racing on Sunday?"

"No, and he's not going to let it get started."

"Now there's a busy lawman," said Ferrine admiringly. "And a mighty smart one. Takes care of the important things first. Well, if you'll excuse me, I'd better be getting along."

He went out onto the sidewalk.

Henry was sitting on a pile of pine-boxed freight on the station platform, studying Main Street through a pair of old lensless army binoculars, when Ferrine came up to her. Her skeletal little figure in its saggy black cotton stockings and patched calico dress was so wispy and frail that a surge of love came over Ferrine and he wished she belonged to Ann and him. She lowered the glasses, made her face as ugly mean as she could, and said, "Lost agin, eh? What you doin' in Farley?"

Ferrine said, "You get smart with me, and I'll snap my handcuffs on you."

"You mean you'd try," she said. "Something I meant to ask you last time I talked to you. You married?"

"Yes, indeed," said Ferrine.

"Happily?"

"Yes, indeed."

She looked nauseated. "Well, if that's what you want, that's what you got."

"That's what I've got."

"I'm never goin' to get married," she announced.

Looking sympathetic, Ferrine said, "I'm sorry to hear it. Why? What's wrong with you?"

"There's nothing wrong with me!" she yelled. Controlling herself, she said, "I can't abide humans. If this subject is too deep for you, we'd better change it."

"Good," said Ferrine. "Because I want to ask you a question. First, I want to thank you for your telegram about Gila Bend. Then I want to ask you this. That telegram your father sent to this Sunset Joe Grenada, at Theba. You say it was signed with a scribble nobody could read. How did he sign the copy he sent? He had to sign it some way, didn't he?"

"He just signed it 'signature unreadable.' That means the signature was unreadable."

"Who sent it, Henry?" asked Ferrine in a low confident voice. "I bet you know everything that goes on in this town. Who would you say really sent it?"

"I don't know," she said, and he completely believed her. "And I wish I did. Because I think it was them, the four fellers the telegram was about, that killed Sheriff Anders."

"So do I," said Ferrine. "But you better never say that again."

"I won't," she said, dry mouthed. Then back in her old self again, she said, "I won't, but let 'em come. They'll wish they hadn't. I'll learn 'em their A-B-C's, goddammit."

Sheriff Lumsden's office, on the second floor of the courthouse, didn't look, to Ferrine, too unlike the office of the Feed, Lumber and Fencing office back in S-burg. No rifle racks or cell bars, just sticky green paint on the walls and a big rolltop desk, its pigeonholes jammed with little packets of paper tied up with string. Sheriff Lumsden sat at his desk, on a pad of folded red stair carpeting, a pen in his hand, practicing arm-movement writing and fancy capitals on a sheet of paper in front of him.

The room was a corner one, and Ferrine stood at a window, looking down into the empty square. Lumsden said, "I heard you were visiting us? May I inquire as to the occasion?"

His smugness and stupidity irritated Ferrine. *What the hell*, thought Ferrine, *let's jolt him a little*. He said, "I wouldn't want to state it definite, but I thought I might come up here to Farley and buy."

"Buy what?"

"A house. A little rose-growed cottage. With a well and an old oaken bucket, a moss-covered bucket and such."

Sheriff Lumsden looked startled, and not too pleased. He said, "It's too dry here for moss-covered buckets. I don't think you'd like it here. And what about your lawing?"

"I'm tired of it. I'd retire. I'd put a little sign in my parlor window, like doctors do, that said Sheriff Wm. Ferrine, Retired. To keep people with law problems away."

"That would just bring 'em," said Lumsden, his face turkey red in outrage. "Farley, would have two sheriffs, me and you."

"They can read in Farley, can't they? It would say *retired*."

"They'd read the sheriff part, too, and that would whet 'em up. I'm afraid I can't permit it. I think they's an ordinance agin it."

"Well, I wouldn't want to break any ordinances," said Ferrine. "Listen, Commissioner Lumsden —"

"Sheriff Lumsden," corrected the other.

"I want a little information. Is Miss' Sophy Cloud in hardship? Naturally, I'd like to help if she is."

"I wouldn't say there's no need of anything along that line."

"Did her husband leave her a sufficient estate?"

"The fact is, I wondered the same and looked it up. He surrogated her that place out there, which you've seen. It might not seem much, but her neighbor does fine. 'Course, they got three times as much land and about six times as many cows."

"What neighbor is that?"

"The Half Circle S, owned by a Powder River syndicate, I understand, up in Montana. Managed by a man named Opperson down at Harrington."

"Harrington," said Ferrine. "I've been in and out of that town several times, but can't really say I know it. It's in Curtis County, isn't it, just over the line, out of — what did you call it? — your diocese?"

"I didn't say diocese. That's for a bishop, not a sheriff, I think."

"I remember now. You said franchise."

"Bailiwick is the word, or jurisdiction. Yes, thank goodness, Harrington is outside my jurisdiction."

"Why do you say thank goodness?"

"Curtis County is so poor and unsightly."

"And you wouldn't want to be sheriff of *that*."

"Who would?"

The hitching rack in front of Aunt Mary's rooming house was an unbarked post with a small tin pie pan spiked down over its top; the pan was there because some mounts, especially some mules, called "stump-eaters," couldn't resist munching post tops. As Ferrine passed it, on his way to his room to get his valise, he saw there was a horse tied to it, and he gave it a quick automatic scrutiny. It had been traveling. Its brand was a half circle with an *s* under it. Half Circle S. He went by it, into the building, saw the sodden old man was nowhere in sight, laid a silver dollar on the desk, went up the steep stairs and into his room.

He had just stepped from the weak light of the hall into the pitch blackness of the room itself, when a soft raspy voice said, "I'm here on peace and unarmed. Don't go half cocked. I'll light a light."

Ferrine closed the door and turned.

There was a little spluttering of fire as a man scratched a match, and an effulgence of pale yellow as he lit a candle on the table.

Ferrine looked at him hard. He had never seen him before. He was a scrawny dirty man with little darting puckered eyes. He wore what were obviously castoff range clothes bestowed upon him by a variety of persons: mismatched boots with rundown heels, a ragged sweaty shirt, frayed khaki pants, a length of lariat for a belt. He wore no gunbelt.

He sat down on the cot, on the tangle of bedclothes that were exactly as Ferrine had left them. He smiled, and somehow managed to get his tongue into the smile, evilly, as though it were an extra, middle lip.

Ferrine said, "Make it quick. I'm leaving. What can I do for you? Who are you, by the way?"

"Just a wuthless nobody, Sheriff Ferrine. Knowed here and there as Texas Slim."

They stared at each other. The hobo's gaze was relaxed with wicked enjoyment.

"I want to talk to you," said Ferrine.

"I thought you might. I got two things to sell you."

"You're the man that sent the telegram that caused me to kill an innocent person?"

"The same. Sent it, but didn't write it. That's one of the things I'm going to sell you."

"You're not going to sell me anything," said Ferrine, almost inaudibly, knotted in cold rage. "You're going to tell me, of your own free will, and then I'm going to beat you to death. Here. Now."

"Some hold one opinion of such a matter, some holds another," said the drifter, unperturbed. "Ain't you interested in where I been staying since?"

"At the Half Circle S?"

"Right. Ain't you interested in who ambushed Miss' Cloud's boy-hand, Tolliver?"

"Don't tell me you did?"

"Me and the Half Circle foreman, a galoot named Hackberry Tibbs."

"Why?"

"Now I got you interested. Now I got you runnin' up a bill. You're askin' questions. To scare Miss' Cloud."

"Kill an innocent boy to scare an innocent woman," said Ferrine. "For a reason, or just for fun?"

"Here I can't say for sure, but maybe to tender her up. Maybe they want to buy her land. It sticks into their'n like a sore thumb."

"You mean this Powder River company?" asked Ferrine in disbelief.

"I ain't consulted on everything." Now the hobo was wary.

Suddenly, like the snap of a whip, it came to Ferrine that he was being deceived. Not deceived — for he was sure every word he'd listened to had been the truth — but being diverted.

The hobo said, "I hate lawmen worse than manure-worms, Sheriff. I was sent here to kill you."

His right hand had been half curled in his lap, his left listless on the jumbled bedclothes. Now, moist-eyed, he raised his left hand and it held a cut-down pistol-gripped shotgun.

Ferrine nailed him three times with a smokehouse pattern. If you heard someone fooling around your smokehouse at night, and you went to the back door and could see nothing because of the dark, you placed, to your best judgment, three shots around the padlock: one above it, two more farther down, left and right, all of them in a triangle. It was a hard pattern to escape, even when you were shooting blind. The hobo went off the cot and onto the floor as though he were boneless, dead before the third slug hit him.

Ferrine got his valise, put on the candle, and descended the stairs to the entry room. There was no sign of the old man still, probably by arrangement. His silver dollar was still on the desk. He paused, laid a gold coin beside the silver one, and with nearby pen and ink wrote, *The dollar is for rent due on Room 16. The goldpiece is for you if you would please put a bunch of some kind of flowers on Burt Anders' grave.*

As he wrote, he saw an Aunt Mary's bedbug walking along his cuff, and removed it. A fat rat, with stiff bristly brown hair and a pink scaly tail, scampered across the lamp-lit floor behind the desk into shadow.

Swinging his valise, he stepped out into the starry night, leaving nothing but foulness behind him.

He walked toward the station.

CHAPTER
SIX

There were times, on the hottest of hot days, Ferrine had noticed, when the air seemed at the same time both crystal clear and shimmering, and shadows from the sun's blaze were like thin blue gauze. Harrington was that way when he climbed down from the rear coach of the east-bound A. & P. express directly into the middle of the town.

If you could call it a town.

He shifted his valise from one hand to the other, and looked about him. Very close at hand, clustered about him, was the water tank for the locomotives, the little deserted depot, and about a hundred yards of switch track with a couple of lonesome boxcars looking forgotten, lost. In a circle beyond this, without street plan, were maybe twenty houses and shops, sand rasped, weathered, gray. On all sides, almost to the back door of the buildings, were sand and rock rubble, greasewood and mesquite, studded here and there with monstrous boulders and networked with dry stream beds and gullies. Ferrine went into the station, dispatched his valise back to S-burg, and sent a telegram to Annie: *Will be delayed but things going pretty good — Bill*. The stationmaster, marking a sheep hide with a piece of soapstone to fashion a winter vest, didn't much enjoy being interrupted, but grudgingly obliged.

Once again outside in the sun, looking over the crazy patchwork scattering of buildings — sides facing sides, sides half facing backs, back doors facing each other, no real streets or walks, just roadways and paths — looking them over carefully this time, he saw in the near distance a two-story clapboard residence, more pretentious than its neighbors, painted for one thing, painted a faded coffee brown, with a sign across its front which read: L. OPPERSON, LAND & STOCK.

Ferrine wove his way among the sand-whipped rickety buildings, mounted the Opperson front steps and knocked on the Opperson front door.

Ferrine was sure, when he got an eyeful of the mortal that answered, that he was looking at him in person, at the article that styled himself the "Big Man of Harrington."

He was a thick-set brute of a man, vain and domineering in his bearing, maybe in his early forties. He was dressed in dark blue, good cloth, but it was almost greasy stiff from frugal wear. His head and neck were of the same meaty thickness, his eyes seemed encased in little bags of wrinkled leather, and his carroty hair looped down in ringlets over the back of his collar.

"Mr. Opperson?" asked Ferrine, and when he nodded ever so slightly, Ferrine said, "I'm Bill Ferrine, sheriff down at Stantonsburg. I'd like a few minutes' conversation with you if you can spare the time."

"Along what line?" asked Opperson briskly.

"Why do you ask that?"

"I'm a busy man, as I'm sure you are."

"Along the line of T. L. Cloud."

"I've never heard of any T. L. Cloud. Sorry. Good day."

"You heard of him at least five hundred and eighty dollars and no cents worth," said Ferrine mildly. "I've seen a receipt to him for that amount signed by you."

"Come in," said Opperson, stepping back so that Ferrine could enter.

As they walked halfway down a short hall and turned through a door, Ferrine said, "I wouldn't call that getting off to a good start for us. If you're not honest with me, it could get me into a mess of trouble and, who knows, might get you into a little, too." His tone was dispassionate, casual.

Opperson said, "I don't like threats."

They were in a comfortable little room, whitewashed, Indian cured animal hides on the bare yellow floor, Apache war gear, shields, lances, leather quivers on the walls. Two cavalry sabers were crossed on a Yaqui blanket hung over the roughstone fireplace. *A man that's ex-military*, thought Ferrine, *or more likely a man who sort of hopes you'd think he's ex-military.* Opperson gestured to a thong-bottomed chair, but Ferrine shook his head and remained standing. He didn't like his host and refused to be beholden to him in any degree. He wouldn't even sit. There was a moment of silence. The air was stuffy. Opperson, who had changed in his manner entirely and was now affable, said, "Drink?"

Ferrine rebuffed him insultingly by ignoring the invitation completely. He said, "You know, I have a feeling you've suddenly remembered my party."

"Cloud? I remembered him all along. But his business with me is confidential."

Ferrine said, "He's dead."

"Dead? What happened to him?"

"Accident," said Ferrine. "You don't seem disturbed."

"Why should I be?" said Opperson. "I was just calculating. He was always conscientious in paying his way as he went along. Our accounts must be absolutely even, to the penny."

"And that's your only worry, the money end of it?"

"What else is there? If you mean the other thing, the demise-dust we art to dust returneth. What did you want to ask me about him?"

"How many cows you sold him."

"None."

"None?" said Ferrine. "What did you sell him?"

"Nothing."

"Nothing? Then what was your business with him?"

Opperson considered a moment, then said, "All right. Here it is. He was supporting a certain person here in Harrington. I'd see to the paying of her rent, and that she had proper food, and so on, and he'd settle with me. He wished his name kept out of it. Our arrangement was that I work as sort of a trustee, for a fee. You'd be surprised at the variety of dealings I'm engaged in."

"I'm sure beginning to. So Cloud was keeping a woman here?"

"Not the kind of woman you have in mind. This is his sister."

"Then why all around Robin Hood's barn to do it?"

"All I know about it is what he said, which was very little. They weren't on speaking relations with each other, and she wouldn't take any charity from him. Maybe he beat her out of the family inheritance or something and later got sorry."

"Did she think the money came from you?"

Opperson smiled. "How do I know what she thought? But she sure as hell took it."

"Did she know where her brother was?"

"We never talked about that."

"Well, well," said Ferrine. "What is this lady's name? How do I find her?"

"She lives across town, north of the water tank, in a shanty," said Opperson. He described the shanty and gave directions for locating it.

Ferrine thanked him, and left. He didn't mention any Powder River cattle company, or the Half Circle S.

It wasn't a shanty, and no one but a snob like Opperson would have called it one. Some people might have called it a hut, but to Ferrine it was just a small house. Under the roof of its little porch, suspended on lengths of darning thread or string, from taut overhead wires, were bunches of weeds, sun-drying. As Ferrine drew closer, he saw they weren't weeds, exactly, but herbs, medicinal herbs, of the sort his mother always used. A card on the front door said, *Cousin Jenny. Midwifery. Home remedies. Nursing.*

For "midwifery" read also abortions, thought Ferrine, and knocked. Somehow, unreasonably, a great distaste was growing in him.

To the woman who opened the door, lank, middle-aged, stone-faced, and dressed in starched slate-gray muslin, he said, "Miss Cloud?"

"I'm Cousin Jenny," she said. "What do you want?"

"Mr. Luke Opperson told me that I could find you here," said Ferrine. "I've bad news. Mr. T. L. Cloud is dead." He didn't like her, but he tried to speak as gently as possible.

"I know he's dead," she said. She was completely unmoved. "I saw it in the *Farley Telegraph*." The hard grayness of her face almost matched the grayness of her dress.

Over her shoulder, he could see a little section of her living quarters: a third of a sooty fireplace, the foot of a bed, white linen and brass knobbed footposts — her bed; and an ugly looking trestle-cot covered with a black india rubber blanket — the bed for her agonized patients. Ferrine averted his eyes.

He said, "You read it in the *Farley Telegraph?* I've just this minute talked to Mr. Opperson. He didn't know about it. I wonder why he didn't see it."

"He did," she said. "He was the one that showed it to *me*."

Ferrine thought this over.

"Anything else?" she asked.

61

"I should tell you I was the one who killed him," he said.

She nodded. Absently. As though he had merely passed on the time of day to her. He could hardly believe it. Then her manner dismissed it. She reached behind her into the room, and her hand came out with a lumpy fishnet bag. She hung the bag with the herbs, also to sun-dry. It contained small animal, probably rabbit, viscera. More home cures.

He muttered a brief goodbye, and walked away.

Flies were already collecting on the bag.

Diagonally across from the depot, across a couple of dozen yards of iron-dry ground, was a general store, false-fronted in weathered pine, saying in big letters: SCHAUM'S. There was a loading platform about tailgate high across its front, and Ferrine deduced it must do most of its trade with outlying ranches. There were stores like this, that specialized in range trade; they stocked supplies to fit it, and customers, range folk, always made them their social and meeting headquarters on town visits. At the moment, there was a wagon, just one, backed up to the platform. It was a light general utility work wagon, of the type known as "plantation" wagons. A sawed-off hammered down gray mule was hitched to it, and as Ferrine came up he saw the mule bore a Half Circle S brand.

He was on the platform when two men came out of the store wrestling a big spool of barbwire between them, and having difficulty. Spools of wire could be unwieldy. Without being asked, he stepped forward and helped them stow it in the wagon. Their action, finished, left them standing in a little circle, their boot toes almost touching, grinning at each other, and panting.

One was the storekeeper: you could tell that from his apron. The other was a cowhand. This one, about Ferrine's age, was a large slumpy man with a pocked face and giant hands all gristle and horny callus. He wore wristbands of heavy leather, extending almost to his elbows, and the chin cord to his flat-crowned hat was of natural horsehair, neatly and skillfully braided: bunkhouse work maybe; cell work maybe. The storekeeper said, "I'm Schaum. This-here is Mr. Hackberry Tibbs. We thank you."

"Glad to meet both of you gentlemen," said Ferrine. "I'm Bill Ferrine. The man that's got them fooled into thinking he's their sheriff down the track at Stantonsburg."

The man Tibbs looked utterly — but politely — unconcerned. This had to be the foreman of Half Circle S, the one Texas Slim had said was in on the ambushing of Mrs. Cloud's hand, the boy Tolliver. The storekeeper said, "We're honored. May I ask what brings you to our metropolis?"

"I just had a little visit with one of your leading residents," said Ferrine. "A gentlemen named Opperson."

"You wouldn't take it unmannerly of me if I asked what about?" said the storekeeper.

"Ask a sheriff a question like that," said Tibbs, "an' you'll get your ears chewed off." He spoke good-humoredly.

"Breeder-bulls," said Ferrine. "A man I know down at S-burg, Mr. Mike Ross, asked me if my travels took me through Harrington to have a word with Opperson On the subject. Mr. Ross deals in breeder-bulls."

Hackberry Tibbs relaxed slightly; Ross was known in three counties in this capacity.

"So you're just traveling through," said Tibbs. "That's understandable. A lawman does a lot of travelin'."

"Travelin' through to where?" asked the gossipy, inquisitive storekeeper.

"To a place maybe fifty miles from here," said Ferrine. "Up near the Mazatzal Range. An outfit run by a Mrs. Cloud. I doubt if either of you have ever heard of it."

"I've heard of it," said Hackberry. "In fact I foreman the spread on the nigh side of it, the Half Circle S. I don't see no horse. How do you aim to get there?"

This was the time to be careful and not over-eager. Ferrine said, "I'll find a way."

"Is that the way you travel?" said the storekeeper, startled. "Leaving it up to luck. Saying, 'I'll find a way'?"

"Is that the way you got here to Harrington?" asked Hackberry.

"I'm afraid I was just joking," said Ferrine. "Here's the way I'm doing it. I got on the train at S-burg and had my horse shipped straight through by rail to Farley. Passing through Harrington, I got off. I'll now go on by rail to Farley, pick up my mount, and go on out to the Cloud place by mount."

They thought this over.

After a moment, Tibbs said, "How about this? Ride along with me an' my barbwire to the Half Circle S, an' give me a little company. After I get my stuff unloaded, I'll drive you over to the place you're headed for."

"That's a mighty kind offer, and I'd relish it," said Ferrine, making a show of deliberately creating difficulties. "But wouldn't that leave me horseless, stranded, at the Clouds'?"

"They'd be glad to make you the loan of a mount back to Farley, where you could leave it for them at the livery stable," said Tibbs, now openly urging him.

"It'll be a pleasure to take you up on it," said Ferrine, and climbed up into the off side of the seat of the plantation wagon.

An hour later, they were well out of town, winding their way through a tangle of chasms and cañons, which Tibbs seemed to know like the palm of his hand. The heat reflected from the stone walls across them in smothering pulsations. Neither Ferrine nor his companion did much talking. Once, Tibbs had said, "It gets better a little later," and that was all.

No conversation, yet Ferrine was sure he had been brought along to be pumped.

Just at dusk, the cañons sloped off into hard scrabble plateau, with a little grass and a few cows. Better grass and more cows would come soon, Ferrine decided. Tibbs said, "We're on Half Circle S land now. It's a monstrous range. We should be at headquarters about noon tomorrow." He pointed at a small log building. "A line camp of our'n. How about eatin' an' spendin' the night there?"

"Whatever you say," said Ferrine. "Suits me fine."

Tibbs reined up before the little structure. "Before we light," he said, "I want to ask you a question, if you won't get gun-hasty on me. You was the one who killed Texas Slim in Aunt Mary's rooming house in Farley, wasn't you?"

"You mean the gent with the cut-down shotgun? Yes, I was. To the best of my recollection."

"You must be pretty quick."

"He should have had it at full cock. Sometimes it isn't a race in hand speed but gun-action, in the gunlock."

"That's right," said Tibbs, vaulting to the ground. "I whet mine down with a razor oilstone."

"I'm not that careful, I guess," said Ferrine. "I generally make my own oilstone with a chunk of limestone and a dab of lard."

"Well, you saved me a job. I was about all set to do it myself."

"How did you know it was me?"

"Just come over me like a revelation. Slammed into me like a bolt of lightning, you might say. Are you after me, too?"

"How do I know? I just met you."

"Well, let's get something together to eat, an' eat it," said Hackberry Tibbs. "I'm hungrier than a mamma puma with a litter o' nine."

CHAPTER
SEVEN

The real inquisition, carefully played out, sometimes with heavy joviality, sometimes with mock sobriety, came at the plank table in the lamplight, over the coffee cups, about an hour later. It was Annie's theory that a man who asks questions tells you more than he asks, and Ferrine's theory, too, so he took the whole thing as seriously as though he were in a courtroom. He wasn't afraid of his opponent. A man who really whets down his gun-action doesn't run around bragging about it, but keeps it to himself, as an edge. Ferrine was pretty sure this Tibbs was no real gun artist: he worked too hard to give that impression.

Ferrine got in the first question before the barrage from Tibbs, which he knew was coming up. He said, "You claim you, yourself, were all set for this Slim. Why? What did you have against him?"

"I ordered him off the place. An' to tell the truth, I was afraid he'd go into Farley an' tell lies about me."

"What kind of lies?"

"Who knows? But they'd be harmful; he was lower'n a snake."

"How did you get tied up with him in the first place?" asked Ferrine.

"Don't put it that way. I was never 'tied up with him.' He wandered onto the Half Circle S drivelin' an' starved and I fed him and garmented him an' give him a corner of the mow wherein to lie his weary head. He stayed with us for a while an' then the boys in the bunkhouse began missing little things (which we traced to him) an' I ordered him off the premises. He was lucky they didn't loop a rope around his neck."

"I wonder why he was waiting for me at Aunt Mary's," said Ferrine.

"We'll never know. That'll always be one of the great mysteries o' life, I guess."

Ferrine rolled a neat little cigarette of rice-paper and flaked home-grown twist, lit it, and glanced around him, sizing up his surroundings. It was a typical line camp: small stove, double bunks, side of bacon hanging in a corner, cheesecloth over a small high shelf of other food — probably flour, salt, coffee, maybe a flask of syrup sweetening.

He said, "Before he was taken dead, this Texas Slim told me that you and him ambushed a boy named Tolliver from Miss' Cloud's ranch, missed the boy but got his horse. Of course what happens back by the Mazatzals is more your business than mine, but naturally it got my curiosity up. Why?"

"Did he say that?" exclaimed Tibbs in indignation. "The boy will probably lie an' say that, too, but that's exactly what I was talking about. The boy ambushed me."

"On their land or your land?"

"On their land, it so happens. I was taking a shortcut."

"Bad feeling between the two places?"

"Don't see each other often, but couldn't be friendlier," said Tibbs, and leaned back, flaccid cheeked. *Now come the questions, the reason for the free ride*, Ferrine decided; *now comes the sausage grinder.*

Tibbs said, offhand, "What takes you to the Cloud place?"

"Breeder-bulls," said Ferrine.

"Like Opperson?"

"Breeder-bulls is all I'm privileged to say."

"All at once the world seems full of breeder-bulls," said Tibbs.

"They got that way about them, haven't they?" said Ferrine genially. "As a matter of fact, it's in connection with, adjunct to, and interdependent upon, *per se*, the Opperson situation. Further, I dast not say. There's too much spondulicks involved."

"I ain't pryin' into Mr. Opperson's finances," said Tibbs hastily. "God forbid." He batted his eyes. "Sheriff Burt Anders was a friend o' your'n?"

"Yes."

"He's dead."

"He's dead, but I'm not."

"I wonder who them fellers was that killed him."

"Four gunfighters from the south, brought up just for the job. A Sunset Joe Grenada, from Theba, and three of his friends from Gila Bend."

Tibbs' lips stiffened, but his eyes remained merry and slippery. He said, "I've heard of this Sunset Joe, but

I've never saw him. I wonder what Burt Anders was into, an' who brought them up to work on him."

"Your guess is as good as mine," said Ferrine.

"I wonder where they stayed when they were up here," said Tibbs.

"Somewhere in Farley, I'd say," answered Ferrine. "Maybe even at Aunt Mary's rooming house. It would be a waste of time trying to find out. Gentlemen-on-the-gun are foxes at covering their tracks."

This satisfied Tibbs completely. He was replete. Ferrine could see him ease off his tension. He had learned everything he had wanted to learn. In genuine comradeship, he said, "I got a little croup elixir out in the wagon. Two-X."

"Croup medicine?"

"If you have it, it'll cure you. If you don't have it, it'll give it to you."

"Maybe a couple of fingers," said Ferrine cheerily. "Then I've got to hit that bunk. I hardly know what I'm saying. I'm out like a lamp."

"I thought so," said Tibbs, suppressing his double meaning. "One bottle croup medicine coming up!"

The sun was at its noonday zenith next day when they drove up to the Half Circle S ranch house, and they drove into a remarkable scene. Since dawn they had been penetrating good grass and good herds; better than good, in fact, fine. Ferrine recalled how fine the Cloud grass had been, too, and how wrong Burt Anders had been in underrating it. Always in the background were the Mazatzals. During this leg of the journey,

70

Ferrine and Hackberry chatted sporadically, easily and with little effort, as naturally, anyhow, as two habitually taciturn men could chat. Hackberry had put Ferrine down as harmless and maybe a little stupid. Ferrine, on his part, was now dead certain that the four killers from the south had hidden out at the Half Circle S while they accomplished their job on Anders. If Half Circle S was involved in the mess, did that mean it stopped with Hackberry Tibbs, or that it went on up the ladder to Opperson? It was Ferrine's feeling that it went on up to Opperson. Ferrine didn't know anything at all about that Powder River syndicate that Sheriff Lumsden said actually owned the spread — Opperson just managing for them, he'd said — but it went against his grain to think of a big company indulging in such tactics. And what on earth had Burt Anders discovered that brought about his death?

He and Hackberry had eaten their breakfast in the line camp cabin, washed their dishes and tidied up their bunks for the next man, and set out in the chill pleasant dawn. For about eight straight hours, from the summer sunrise to a little after midday, they passed no habitation.

Coming up out of a grassy swale, they saw the first house, and it was the Half Circle S place, their destination. It was a drab scene. The house itself wasn't much, and the buildings behind it, cookhouse, bunkhouse, barns, sheds and workshops, were rickety and bare, some of them even leaning a little, or sagging; but this part of Arizona was hard on buildings as well as men and animals and you couldn't judge the place's affluence from their condition. Ferrine judged it from the number of buildings, even if they seemed to be falling apart. He judged it to be good. He judged the Half Circle S to be a money maker.

A small knot of people was gathered behind a big decrepit barn.

Hackberry drove up to, and into the gathering, and reined to a stop. Five Half Circle S hands, who had been working in the vicinity, had left their jobs and assembled to see what was going on. Three of them leaned their shoulder blades against the maroon barnside, one leaned on a pitchfork, and another held a double-bitted ax loosely in his arm crook; all of them seemed amused, all of them were watching. They were watching a woman in their midst, a woman in a homemade buckboard, a pair of wheels at the back, another at the front, with four twelve-foot planks between them, resting directly on the axles; the seat was an old buggy seat. The woman in the seat was Miss' Sophy Cloud, barefooted as usual, her face mild and absolutely without expression. In her lap, across the knobby bumps in her dress which were her knees, lay a rifle. It lay there seemingly forgotten. As though someone had put it there and said, "I'll be back and get it in a minute."

It was a '76 Centennial, using a .45-75-305 cartridge, and looked fat in her thin bony fingers.

When Mrs. Cloud saw Ferrine, she said, "Morning, Sheriff. What are you doing in this pig sty?"

"I'm heading for your place," he said. "In a roundabout way."

"Roundabout is correct," she said.

Hackberry looped his reins around the whip socket, and climbed down.

The thing that bothered Ferrine was that she hadn't brought her hands, Layton and Tolliver, along with her.

She said, "Hackberry, I've been dreaming about you. You killed one of my horses. Just lay his price on the ground and start running."

"Don't talk foolish, ma'am," he said gallantly. She shot him through the shoulder.

The gun roared through the barnyard like someone had blasted a stump.

Tibbs reeled, but he stayed on his feet. He didn't draw. He simply grimaced in pain and shock. Two of the bystanders leaning against the barn drew, however. But, guns in their hands, they didn't seem to know what to do with them.

Mrs. Cloud shot Hackberry again, this time in the thigh. He staggered against a wagon bed, slumped against a snubbing post, and started off at a roll, a gout of blood gathering on his chin, his ankles slewing out in jerky spasms. Even now, he didn't draw on her. Even now, the men against the barn, weapons in their hands, did nothing.

Ferrine stared at them. It was physically impossible for any of them to break the code of their fathers and woman-shoot. She knew that, of course. That was why she had left Layton and the boy Tolliver at home; they would have been mincemeat by now.

Deliberately, she let loose a short volley rapidly, aiming carefully. A slug ripped Hackberry's throat to shreds, as though from an inner explosion. Two more pounded into his inner abdomen. Half the crown of his head went off with another.

He fell, withering terribly, and died with a bowel movement.

To the hypnotized Half Circle S hands, she said, "Why don't you rush in to disarm me?"

They stood frozen.

To Ferrine, she said, "Hop in. I'm drivin' home."

Ferrine climbed up beside her and she drove off.

A little later, she said, "Mr. Layton will have supper waiting for us. He's a good cook when the spirit moves him."

The sun slipped down the sky toward the crests of the mountain range. They passed the little creek where Tolliver had gun-slammed Ferrine into unconsciousness that day; the event seemed long, long ago.

"Even if Hackberry paid me the money for the horse of mine he killed, the one Tolliver was riding when he was ambushed," said Miss' Sophy abruptly, "I was aiming to shoot him anyways, and with pleasure."

"Is that so?" said Ferrine warily. "May I be so bold as to inquire why?"

"I wouldn't be surprised if he was the one that sent that telegram to you that got my husband killed," she said.

"I don't think so," said Ferrine.

"Well, I know one thing. The next day, before I'd heard of it, before you and Sheriff Anders come to me, him and Texas Slim rode over from Half Circle S to visit me. Just to see me suffer. But like I said, nobody had brought me the news yet."

"And they themselves didn't mention it?"

"Would you, in their places?"

"Maybe they didn't know it."

"Oh, they knew it, all right. They done it. They came to see me with a broke heart."

"What did they do while they were there at your place?"

"That's how I know. They did absolutely nothing but make up silly excuses for coming. Hackberry rode out with me about six miles west of my barn, where he said he thought he'd seen sign from an Apache war party. And was he disgusted and puzzled and all of that when he couldn't never locate it again."

"There hasn't been a war party through here for years," said Ferrine. "And won't be ever again, I'd say."

"I know it. He was just trying to scare me. To soften me up."

"Soften you up for what?"

"Half Circle S has been wanting to buy my land."

Ferrine said, "You and Hackberry rode out. What became of Texas Slim?"

"He borrowed a hammer from me," said Mrs. Cloud, "and some brads, and stayed back on my doorstep to cobble a bad boot he had."

"And where were Mr. Layton and Tolliver all this time?" asked Ferrine.

"Up in the foothills cutting locust fence posts."

It was early gloaming when they reached the Cloud house. The first thing they saw as they approached was a yellow-spoked buggy tied up out front to the hitching rail.

"Sheriff Lumsden from Farley," said Miss' Sophy.

Ferrine said, "Hold steady. He can't possibly have heard."

Miss' Sophy lighted from the buckboard and entered the house by the back door. Ferrine drove into the barn, unharnessed, fed, and curried down the horse. Then he made his way to the house, and knocked at the kitchen door; Tolliver called, "Come in," and he entered.

They were all sitting around the kitchen table, Sheriff Lumsden, Mrs. Cloud, Tolliver, and Mr. Layton, eating. By each plate was a glass of buttermilk, and in the center of the table was a big glass pitcher of buttermilk. Also on the table — cooked and served by Mr. Layton — were bowls and platters of food, heaped so high as to be startling, dry hash (as opposed to a soupy something known locally as just "hash"), buttered beets, buttered carrots, buttered biscuits the size of teacups, and prune-and-rice pudding.

Layton and Tolliver greeted him with tight little smiles of true welcome. Ferrine took a seat. They began handing him platters and bowls. He served himself. He was all at once ravenously hungry. Sheriff Lumsden cleared his throat, took a big quaff of buttermilk, and said, "I thought you went home, back to S-burg."

"I got sidetracked," said Ferrine respectfully, as though the answer explained everything.

"What brings you here?" asked Sheriff Lumsden.

"I came with Mrs. Cloud," said Ferrine. "What brings *you* here? You get sidetracked, too?"

"I come a-purpose," said Sheriff Lumsden pompously. "I rarely never get sidetracked nowheres."

"That's the way to be," said Ferrine in admiration. "What purpose?"

"I've got information for the people here."

"Well, you're the bishop and this is your diocese," said Ferrine. "I see no reason why you shouldn't roam around to your heart's desire."

With the tine at the edge of his fork, Sheriff Lumsden dragged a wisp of meat from his hash and put it on the rim of his plate. He made quite a business of it. His face was severe. He wanted everyone to know he was suddenly becoming official, that the interval of mere sociability was over and done with.

Pointing to the small fragment, he asked, "Is this-here veal?"

"Yearling," said Layton shortly. "You always ask the age of the meat you eat?"

"Butcher it yourself?"

"Myself," said Layton aggressively. "From our own beef, if that's what you're working your way around to. From our North Meadow herd."

"I believe I'd make a little note of such from now on," said Sheriff Lumsden. "You might have to settle for it later."

"Settle for it?" said Miss' Sophy. "What do you mean by that?" She was so mad she could hardly speak.

"It's chattels. It goes into the estate," explained Sheriff Lumsden.

"Who in the hell do you think I am?" asked Miss' Sophy. "I *am* the estate. I'm Mrs. T. L. Cloud!"

"The mannerly and polite refers to you as such, of course," said Sheriff Lumsden sympathetically. "But I'm thinking of the real Mrs. T. L. Cloud. The lady he married via preacher and all, sixteen years ago. Which he never canceled."

CHAPTER
EIGHT

Everyone was appalled. Even Sheriff Lumsden looked morose.

The silence was horrifying. Miss' Sophy broke it. She said, "I wonder what that makes me?"

After another silence, a shorter one this time, Sheriff Lumsden said boisterously, "Why, it makes you his housekeeper!"

"It makes me his hurdy-gurdy girl," said Miss' Sophy.

No one felt like laughing, though they all looked at her.

"When did this happen?" asked Ferrine.

"This morning," said Sheriff Lumsden. "She came into my office about ten o'clock."

"Who came in?" asked the grizzled Mr. Layton.

"Mrs. Cloud. Pardon me, Mrs. Cloud," said Sheriff Lumsden. "Until the courts okay it, nacherally I'm neither here nor there, personally. But they'll pass it, Mrs. Cloud, in favor of Mrs. Cloud. They ain't much doubt of that."

They sat in moody gravity.

"If Mr. T. L. was alive," said Sheriff Lumsden ponderously, "I do believe this would make him a common-law bigamist — and you don't scarcely ever hear of one of *them*."

"When we come to this place," said Miss' Sophy, "they wasn't nothing but nothing. We, him and me, put our shoulders together like a yoke o' oxen and made something of it. I built about half of this house myself, with my own bare hands, and now she wants to take it away from me."

"Why don't you send her a bill for it?" asked Sheriff Lumsden helpfully. "And maybe a bill for that other, too, the housekeeping?"

But not at hurdy-gurdy girl rates, thought Ferrine.

"Possession is nine-tenths of the law," said Miss' Sophy aggressively.

"Not when that other tenth wears a badge," said Sheriff Lumsden regretfully. "I don't want to have to come out here with a posse and eviction papers and writs and warrants and all. But we'll cross that bridge when we come to it. I'm sure you're going to be reasonable, Mrs. Cloud. I got a feeling that Mrs. Cloud is going to be reasonable. In her nice quiet ladylike way, all she seems to want is to get her talons around that lucre, so to speak."

"Reasonable?" said Miss' Sophy. "What worse could she do?"

"She could sue you for alienation of affections," said Sheriff Lumsden. "Not that I would, was I her. But I just throwed that in to show you how well off you was."

"What proof did this lady offer?" asked Ferrine.

"She had the kind of proof the law accepts," said Lumsden. "She had a printed marriage certificate wedding T. L. Cloud to her and —"

"T. L.?" said Ferrine. "That doesn't sound legal. What do the T and L stand for? The whole name goes on a contract."

"The T. L. was an initial name," said Lumsden. "That's all there was. It's legal enough. She had this certificate, signed by a parson named Clifford. She had a letter from the parson's wife, Mrs. Clifford, wrote to her later calling her Mrs. Cloud, and asking if she dast put nonalcoholic almond extract in her fruit cake instead of brandy, and how was Mr. T. L. making out. They was living over in Colorado at the time; later, they separated, each going their separate ways, him to Farley, her to Harrington. He supported her, though, in fits and starts, even though they weren't living together. And she had the Johnson family Bible, with the section on Johnson births and deaths and marriages. With the event in it: Jennifer Johnson, married to T. L. Cloud, dated sixteen years ago, over in Colorado."

Ferrine said, "Jennifer Johnson? Harrington?"

"That's where she lives now, Harrington," said Lumsden. "She's a sort of nurse there. Knowed under the name of Cousin Jenny."

When the meal was finished, Miss' Sophy made a formal little speech, very brief. She almost gagged on the words, yet in a bulldogged way she went through with it and even managed to get some false cordiality into it and a feeling of hospitality. She said, "I'm afraid night has come down on us, Sheriff Lumsden. Why

81

don't you and Sheriff Ferrine spend the night with us in our guest room? The both of you can go back to Farley in the morning. I'll lend Sheriff Ferrine a horse, and he can leave it at the livery stable there."

"Thank you kindly," said Lumsden decisively. "But I got to be getting back to town, starting as of now. I'm a man pretty much in demand and I may be needed any time."

"Drive at night?" said Layton, shaking his head in pretended concern. "I don't mean to spook you, but that's when most lawmen vanishes forever from the world of men, at night. At night, on lonely roads."

"I've did it before," said Lumsden, not too enthusiastically. "And besides, that's what I'm paid for, to take enormous risks. Mr. Ferrine, I understand you're headed for Farley, too. Would you like to ride along with me in my buggy?"

"I'd be pleased to," said Ferrine.

"Why do you call him *Mr.* Ferrine?" asked Tolliver. "Down at S-burg, he's Sheriff Ferrine."

"That's down at S-burg," explained Lumsden.

To Tolliver, Layton said patiently, "Well you asked him, and he told you."

Lumsden, Tolliver, and Layton left the kitchen and went out front.

Miss' Sophy, alone with Ferrine, said, "What's going to happen? About me and Hackberry." She looked grim. "Not that I wouldn't do it all over again the same way, if I had the chance."

"I wouldn't worry too much about Hackberry," said Ferrine. "Half Circle S started it, with their ambush of

Tolliver. My guess is that they don't want to cause too much stir. They'll bury him, and if they ever come up with a story at all, it'll be a pretty harmless one. Maybe you and me won't even be mentioned."

"But how did you feel about it? I mean you, yourself?"

"It was sufficient unto my satisfaction."

She inspected his face slowly through her slit eyes. "How come?"

"You might have saved me a job."

She tried to read his thoughts through his irises.

He said, "I mean sooner or later, I might have come to it myself."

She stood there, listening.

He said, "I came into my room in a Farley rooming house not too far back, and Texas Slim was sitting on my bed, waiting to shotgun me."

"And you killed him first?"

"Yes."

"I heard about the death, and wondered."

"There was nobody in that room but him and me. Even the old man that runs the place was gone when I came downstairs."

She said nothing.

Ferrine said, "Yet last night, when me and Hackberry ate and bunked alone in a Half Circle S line camp, he brought the subject up. He knew about it. That means he was either in on it, or even was the one who ordered it. My death . . . Did Opperson ever come here?"

"Never."

"Nonetheless, I think Opperson is behind it all."

"Behind the death of T. L., too?"

"Could be."

"Behind the death of Burt Anders?"

"He'll regret it, if he was."

They left the kitchen, went down the hall, out the front door into the hot night.

They joined the others at the buggy. Lumsden hefted himself to the seat, and picked up the reins. Ferrine took the place beside him. Tolliver unhitched, and stepped back. The vehicle was drawn by a span of beautifully matched mares — one more than was necessary. The rubber tires on the high wheels were thick and the oversize springs seemed to float Ferrine in the air. Lumsden leaned back luxuriously. He said, "Farley County sheriffs travel in style."

They moved off.

Behind them, Layton bawled, "Don't let no *bandidos* reach out and snatch at you from the dark!"

Lumsden said nervously, "What's wrong with that man? There's nothing to be afraid of, absolutely nothing, sir. Darkness is just a state of mind. Calm yourself."

Ferrine accepted a taxpayer cigar, lit it, leaned back, too, luxuriously, smiling faintly, and calmed himself.

The mildness and fragrance of the cigar were wonderful beyond description. He thought of Annie, and how he'd have to get down to it and fix that cupboard hinge she'd been harping on.

Lumsden, who had been talking all the while, said, "Yes, darkness itself never hurt anybody. But we've got to be sensible about this. I've got sandwiches under the seat. How about eating them here, about midnight,

84

without stopping, just keeping right on until we get there?"

"Suits me," said Ferrine.

When, at midnight, they had munched their sandwiches, wheels rolling, and had swigged them down with the contents of a canteen tasting faintly of rye whisky, Ferrine said, "You know, I didn't understand you back yonder at Miss' Sophy's when you called that marriage certificate a contract."

"Because it was signed by the preacher, a Parson Clifford."

"It's the license that's a contract. And it's signed by the probate judge, or his deputy. That's the thing that's legal. It has information about both parties, and goes on courthouse record. The certificate is just a memento, sometimes just a fancy little book, sometimes a big sheet of paper with gold and silver on it. That's the one that's signed by the parson. He gives it to you to sort of remind you to give something, too. Say a five dollar bill."

"License, certificate, that's splitting hairs."

"Not for a moment, splitting hairs," said Ferrine. "Every preacher has a stock of these. I bet I could buy one in blank, telling the preacher some rigmarole, and fill it out and date it, and even make up a name and sign it myself, and marry you to Geronimo's squaw."

"Don't talk that way," said Lumsden coldly. "And what about the family Bible?"

"Buy a new one and fill it out howsoever the mood took me, or buy an old one and just add a line or two to fit in with the rest."

"The letter?"

"Was it in a envelope with a postmark and canceled stamp?"

"No."

"What was the name of this town in Colorado where they were supposed to have been wedded?"

"She didn't say. But it'll come out in the trial, of course. And there'll be witnesses. Probably the Reverend Clifford himself."

"Witnesses can be bought, cheap. About any Cliffords appearing, I wouldn't want to bet on it."

"You just don't believe it, hey?"

"Am I allowed an opinion? I'm out of my jurisdiction."

"Of course you're allowed an opinion."

"No, I don't believe it. But that's not what worries me."

"What worries you?"

"How a lawyer, if he happens to be vile mouthed, can crucify Miss' Sophy, if he gets her in court."

"If she's done nothing wrong, she's got nothing to be afraid of," said Lumsden. "Oh, you mean that common-law part of it?"

Ferrine didn't bother to answer.

Lumsden said smugly, "Any weekend visit to Farley and a trip to a minister would have put her on the safe side, even if it wouldn't have helped in the long run. We must pay for our oversights. Nothing in life is free."

They reached Farley about nine next morning and Sheriff Lumsden, letting Ferrine out of the buggy at the street corner, and saying he had some extremely critical business to take care of, drove home, ate an omelet of six eggs, skillet-browned quartered onions, and pinto beans and fell into bed, travel exhausted.

Ferrine had a light breakfast at a café, a half order of fried potatoes and two thin slices of rib roast — this was no time to gorge himself, he decided — and went to Trenchard's store. The bed could wait.

If T. L. Cloud got secret mail at Trenchard's, Trenchard could very likely have other information about Cloud, also of a secret nature.

It was a little early in the morning for trade: good wives were at home doing domestic slave labor, as they should be, and good husbands were discussing race horses and passing females and preferences in chewing tobaccos, in front of barbershops and livery stables, as was their proper masculine responsibility. The store, when Ferrine came in from the sun's blaze, seemed cool, dim, and vast. There were a few customers, wandering listlessly, a few clerks, waiting eager eyed, and Mr. Trenchard himself, moving from place to place, aligning things on shelves, reshuffling bolts of yard goods, flecking away imaginary specks of lint, watching everybody, everything, impressive in his soft fawn wool, erect and half bald, calm and distant mannered. He was going to be a hard man to question, a hard man to trick with words.

He came forward, greeted Ferrine pleasantly enough, and said, "Is this of a confidential nature, whatever it is? Would you like to go back to my office, and talk over a drink?"

"No thank you," said Ferrine. "You're a busy man. Me, I'm just ambling around, taking in the sights."

"I bet," said Trenchard, with a little cackle of laughter.

For a short interval neither of them said anything.

Finally, Ferrine said, "All right. I wonder if you'd tell me everything you might know about the late T. L. Cloud. I'm putting this as a request, not a demand."

"I'll go along," said Trenchard, after a moment's consideration. "But your question is too general. You'll have to be more specific."

"Did you know he had a wife in Harrington?"

"No," said Trenchard, endeavoring to conceal his amusement. "He never received any letter from her here. In fact, he never got any letters from anybody, except Mr. Opperson. Light is beginning to dawn! Was Opperson his paymaster to her down there? You know, his agent to pass on a little wherewithal now and then to keep her from coming up here and smashing his status quo?"

"I'm not used to this kind of lingo," said Ferrine. "I'm not sure I get it. You should be talking to my wife, Annie."

"I wonder what Miss' Sophy's got in her mind to do," said Trenchard, suddenly serious.

Probably buy a case of .45-75-305's, thought Ferrine.

However, he said, "How do I know? Maybe take Mr. Layton and Tolliver and start again from scratch up in Montana or Canada or someplace. Maybe this

Harrington wife will settle out of court with Miss' Sophy and agree to stake her."

"I don't see how anyone could settle a thing like that out of court," said Trenchard, for the sake of debate. "By the way, myself and a couple of other gentlemen are due to go out to the place and look things over, and put an official value on it. Appraise it for tax purposes."

"Expect to find it valuable?"

"Never can tell. I'd say better than most think."

"Say I lived in Harrington, and was of the feminine gender," said Ferrine, "and wanted a nice big brass bed. How would I get it?"

"You'd come to Farley here for it, or go down to S-burg," said Trenchard.

"Do you have a customer from there named Miss or Mrs. Jennifer or Jenny Cloud, or Miss or Mrs. Jennifer or Jenny Johnson?"

"No, I don't. She either trades somewhere else in town or down at S-burg. So that's the other woman, eh?"

"I wonder how a town like Harrington ever gets started," mused Ferrine, not getting anywhere, and trying to ease off into safer grounds. "It's nothing."

"Nothing now," said Trenchard. "But from what I've heard it was a little better in time gone by. It was a second-rate railhead for the old Wethersfield-Clark herd trail. The original trail actually started down in Mexico and came north as far as Harrington. The trail's gone now, and the town is almost gone. They tell me there used to be chutes and pens, everything there. Farley and S-burg drained the life out of it."

Ferrine had heard this history many times, but listened as though it were all entirely new to him. He had, in fact, once been down part of the trail.

That was barren, seared, almost uninhabited country. The few settlers were odd folk, antagonistic, hostile to invaders. They were hard (he'd seen chickens killed, not by the nonsense of having their necks wrung, but by simply having their heads pulled off under a boot heel), superstitious (many still believed in the omens and even witchcraft of their distant New England forefathers), and tough (many a man had amputated his own gangrenous finger). And with no medicine but a few herbs or some dried rabbit guts.

Dried rabbit guts. That was the only place in his entire life he had seen that nauseous practice performed. It was not of Yaqui origin, as he had supposed, or maybe Chiricahua, but dawn-age Pennsylvania Dutch.

It came to him in a jarring unshakable conviction. That was where he would have to search, down along the Wethersfield-Clark trail. That was where he would have to backtrack Cousin Jenny.

He left Trenchard and the store, went to the Farley House, got a room, and slept four hours. Waking, he went to the livery stable Anders had recommended, showed his credentials and had no trouble in getting a long-distance, long-time horse and pack mule. He laid in some sketchy camp supplies at an obscure shop, and left town, heading southeast.

Three days later, he was well started southward on the old Wethersfield-Clark.

Four days and many questions later found him still without any information.

CHAPTER
NINE

This was real adobe country, very old, the chalky, crumbling little structures few, gleaming in the sun glare, widely scattered. They stood, a little shabby perhaps, though their builders themselves were long dust. Some had been patched and were still used, as hovels. Some, in the lonesome ranches Ferrine passed, were used as annexes or ells to newer ranch houses; many had become outbuildings or worksheds. The countryside was endlessly dun and bleak. At one period, Ferrine saw and spoke to but two humans in three days.

Yet the longer he traveled, the more convinced he became that somewhere in this sere netherworld lay the answer to his trouble.

The trail itself had vanished from disuse, but in a dozen ways it left its sign, and he had no difficulty in following it. No one he had ever heard speak of it had been certain of its point of origin below the border, some said Chihauhua, some said even Salado, but it was ancient, that was agreed on. Spanish armor and Spanish cannon had passed up along it, likely, years before the first longhorn. Now there was only creosote-bush, agave, pockets of scanty soil, and exposed patches of stony underlay.

He came up to the building about sundown.

It was adobe, three rooms long, one low story high. A veranda, supported by posts, ran its full front length, window and door opening onto it at each room. A woman in a ragged old army tunic and a dirty canvas wagonsheet skirt was sitting on a stool just outside one of the doors, weaving a basket between her straddled knees. Below her skirt hem, her ankle shanks were scaly, gritted with grime; her matted brown hair was streaked with gray.

Ferrine pulled to a halt, and touched his hatbrim politely.

"'Evening," he said. He rested on his saddle horn. "I'm Bill Ferrine, from north a ways. I'm trying to backtrail a female friend of a friend, and it hasn't been easy. She might have been around here some time ago."

"How long ago?"

"Six, eight, ten years. I can't say definite."

These folk, he knew, had long and accurate memories.

He described Cousin Jenny in detail. "She might have been called Miss Johnson. Or Mrs. Cloud. Or about anything, I wouldn't swear."

"Never laid eyes on her or never heard of her," said the woman decisively. "I got some real coffee. Come in and have a cup. And maybe a bite of supper. And maybe spend the night. This-here is a kind of hotel."

So close to the border, and on the old trail, he had a pretty good idea of the kind of a hotel it was, away down here in all this nothing, of the kind of patrons it might shelter.

Well, why not, he thought. "I believe I will, thank you kindly," he said. He dismounted and hitched.

"There's a lean-to out back," she said. "Your creature will be took care of whilst you're eating."

"By who?" asked Ferrine.

"By me," she said. "Who else?"

He followed her inside.

Dusk had fallen. She lighted the yellow-tonged wick of a kerosene lantern. In the interplay of light and shadow, he saw it was a typical adobe room, pole rafters overhead, packed earth underfoot. He sat at a table. She placed a crockery bowl before him, and ladled it brimful of some sort of thick-sauced stew, filled with lumps of meat, and placed a plate of thin hard pancake bread beside it; he wondered what the meat was, and decided he was better off if he didn't know. "I'm sorry it's no better," she said.

"It couldn't be any better," he said, and began to devour it.

There were two doors here, one at the rear of the house, one at Ferrine's left to the inner part of the house.

Now muffled sounds came from behind this second door. "My other customer," said the woman. "He's just getting out of bed. He come up to my door at a gallop, half out of his head with hard ridin', and slept eighteen hours. When he comes in, make out like you don't even see him. I have a feeling that's the way he'd want it."

The man who came into the room was slouchy, vicious-eyed, with a scraggly orange beard about five days old. His face was sun-inflamed. He had been riding hard and long, and dust coated the wrinkles of his clothes, thick as pollen. His holster was thonged low, and he carried a rifle. Of all things, there was a bandolier of rifle cartridges looped over his shoulder. His shirt was open to his waist, showing nakedness to his navel. It was Ferrine's professional guess that he was fleeing from a dispersed gang from below the border, maybe a gang that raided isolated haciendas. He was an ugly proposition. And he would be hair-trigger.

The woman said, "Before you set down, you can pay me my three dollars."

"For what?" said the man scornfully.

"For care of your horse, for two meals and bed for yourself," said the woman. "And that's as reasonable as any kind offer."

"I'll pay you next time by," said the man.

"If you've got it, you pay now," she said. "If you're busted, next time's okay."

"I got it," said the man. "But try to get it."

"You ain't the first toad-frog that ever done me this way," she said. "And God pity you."

"What you aim to do about it?" he asked tauntingly.

"Put out the word."

"To the law?"

"To your friends and mine," she said mildly.

"You don't scare me, you old bitch," said the man nervously, suddenly worried. He reached in his pocket. "You say three dollars?"

"Keep it," she said. "What's did is did. I wouldn't touch it."

Ferrine said, "You don't call a lady a bitch, friend."

He started to get up, and the man's fist hit him.

It must have started from about the floor and caught him, upswing, on his upper lip, driving upward, crashing his nose from the underside up and flat. The stab of pain was terrific, and for the briefest of instants a blackness, a numbness seemed to split his brain. His nostrils gushed, and blood and saliva half choked his gullet. Nevertheless, as the woman told him later, he got to his feet, steadily impassively, a hideous gory sight, kicked the man's rifle from his hand, and knocked him half silly with a tremendous blow to the jaw, just below the ear, one to his belly, and a third, the hardest of all, to his throat. The stranger remained erect, but his eyes were glazed and his knees were spread. Deftly, the woman removed the man's revolver. To Ferrine, she said, "When you play, you don't play penny ante, do you?"

He didn't answer. He said, "What now?"

"You take him out front," she said. "I'll bring his horse around."

Later, when they had him in his saddle, weaving a little, the reins in his hand, and the sensitive horse walking cautiously into the night, the woman said, "Come back inside. We'll have some cookies, a jug of recuperater, and I'll fix that laver-lip o' yours."

"I'm all right," said Ferrine.

"And I'll tell you about Jenny Scanlon," said the woman.

He didn't say, "Who is Jenny Scanlon?" He said instead, "How are you going to fix my lip?"

"With the best cure of all," said the woman. "With dried rabbit guts."

In the kitchen again, across the table from each other in the pleasant watery gold of the lantern, she said, "Jenny Scanlon is no friend o' mine. I think it's best we start, you and me, with a new deck, the truth. Jenny's no kinswoman of yours, is she?"

"No."

"And you're a law officer?"

"Yes."

"A sheriff, I'd say."

"Sheriff it is," said Ferrine. "You're pretty good."

"What do you want her for?"

"I don't want her for anything. I just want to know about her."

"She showed up here ten years ago on a lathered horse. She was from Utah, she said, and why not, they have jails in Utah, too, and she was jailbird to her fingertips. Her name was Jenny Franklin then. She stayed three years, sort of helping me around the place."

Trying to keep all excitement from his voice, Ferrine said, "Then you must have got to know her mighty well."

"As well as anybody ever could, I guess. Her baby was born, died, and buried here."

"Baby?"

"Out behind the lean-to. I can show you, if you're so inclined. Its little homemade headstone is still there."

"Who was its father?"

"Her husband, nacherally. What kind of a place do you think I run?"

"No offense, but maybe they fooled you," said Ferrine. "Did they claim they were married when they came here?"

"They didn't come at the same time. She was here first, and Eagle Tail drifted by six or eight months later."

"Eagle Tail?"

"Eagle Tail Scanlon, so named from the Eagle Tail Mountains, he once told me. He took a fancy to her, she took a fancy to him, so he stayed on. One thing led to another and they began living in the same room together. Ah, me."

Ferrine waited.

"Well, the baby come and died and was buried, like I told you, and I began to get tired of all this scatterbrained folderol and married them."

"*You* married them?"

"Not me personally, o' course," said the woman. "I don't happen to be invested with that particular power. The photographer married them."

Ferrine reached for the jug. "I believe I'll have another drink. Photographer?"

"Part-time photographer, part-time preacher, and part-time sheep dip peddler. So I asked them, Jenny and Eagle Tail, and they said what the hell, sure, and we all got together out front and did it. Eagle Tail, who was heavy with gold, forked out from his money belt, kissed his newly bought merchandise, and we all celebrated.

During the celebrating I learned one thing. Preachers may not drink, but photographers don't seem to know no limit."

Eagle Tail, Eagle Tail. The Eagle Tail Mountains, when you came right down to it, were not *too* far from Gila Bend, and Theba, and Sunset Joe Grenada and his three gun-throwing friends. Not that that *had* to mean anything — but old brotherhoods, old comradeships, hung on.

Ferrine said, "And a little later this bridal couple left, heading north?"

"He left first, he was a nacheral-born deserter." The old woman looked wry. "She left later."

"With a broken heart."

"With my chatelaine watch. And no grief noticeable. I don't know where either of them headed."

"What was his trade?" asked Ferrine.

"Cattle."

"What was hers, if any?"

"None at all when she come here. I taught her a little about herbs."

"Could you describe this Scanlon for me?" urged Ferrine seriously. "This is very important."

"I can do better than that," she said. "I can show you a picture of him."

"A picture!"

"The photographer threw in a free photograph of them, along with the ring. She left the ring, too, if you'd care to see it."

Stunned, he nodded. The woman left the room, was gone a short time, and returned with a blue bandanna handkerchief knotted into a pouch. She untied the knots, and laid out the handkerchief on the tabletop by the lantern.

First he picked up the cheap brass ring and tilted it. Inside, he could see letters: *Thos. Scanlon to his beloved wife Jennifer.*

"Who did this?" asked Ferrine.

"The preacher. He was also a part-time —"

"I know. Engraver. Poor hungry man. All of them no-money professions. No wonder he was a hard drinker."

"Like to take it along with you?"

"No," said Ferrine. "Keep it yourself, but hold on to it." He picked up the photgraph.

It had been taken out in front of the building, as she had said, and, all things considered, was pretty clear. There was the old woman, grinning. There was Cousin Jenny, Midwifery, Home Remedies, Nursing, as distinct as an etching, almost exactly as he had talked to her in Harrington. The third person, the man, had moved a little and was slightly blurred-moved a little on purpose, Ferrine was certain. He was smoking a cigar which he was holding flat-handed across the lower part of his face. You could see the whites of his eyes under his hatbrim. Above his gunbelt he wore a spare cartridge belt, making a lot of belt and a lot of metal for a guileless cowhand to be carrying. There was a touch of vaquero to his clothes — though he sure as heck wasn't a vaquero — a sombrero with little balls dangling from its brim and a Mexican quirt under his left arm. One thing certain, he wasn't T. L. Cloud.

100

"Like I said," declared Ferrine, "I'll leave the ring with you. But I'd like to take this along, if it's okay."

"Help yourself," she said. "But you're not leaving? Just when I've taken a liking to you?"

"I'd better do it while I can," he said. "You South Arizonians are too tough for me."

"So I just noticed," she said. "Well, I'll get your horse and all."

"Listen," he said. "I'm leaving the pack mule and the extra gear that's on it. Please accept them as a gift. I owe you a heap more than that, and I can have a pack animal hold me back from here on in. It's rented, but I'll settle for it at the other end. My home is in S-burg. My wife and me would be mighty pleased to have you look us up and drop in if you ever got up that way."

"I never get no way," she said. "I never have, and don't want to. My folks come here from Pennsylvania in '57, and my skin and bones and soul and heart has growed mighty deep into this hellacious country. Could you understand me if I told you I *love* it?"

"I understand," he said quietly.

She said, "I'll put some food in your saddlebags. Victuals that are healthy for you and will keep on a trip. Ashcake, maybe, and a piece of brined rope."

Wincing, Ferrine said, "Is this brined rope really pickled snake of some kind?"

"Ask me no questions and I'll tell you no lie. I'll also add an extra pair of canteens."

He said, "How long do you say it will take my big lip to heal?"

"A couple of days. If you keep the blowflies off it. It's blowflies that lay the eggs that hatch into maggots."

She started for the back door, for her stable.

He didn't offer to help. He didn't follow her.

He had a feeling that her stable would be very private territory.

When he left, he headed for Farley again, not S-burg and home. About dawn, he stopped, put the mare on a long picket, and camped for a piece of ashcake, a piece of brined rope, a swig of water, and a few hours' sleep.

It was the blistering whip of the sun which woke him. A light breakfast, a light drink from a canteen, and he was again on his way. His sleep had been restless, troubled, utterly unrefreshing. He had the Cousin Jenny question settled. She hadn't been married in Colorado, or anywhere else, likely, to Cloud. She had been long ago married in an outlaw hangout, by a roving photographer-preacher, to a hardcase looking character known, at that moment at least, as Eagle Tail Scanlon; there was a witness, the old woman, a ring, and a baby's grave behind a barn to confirm it. Confronted with all this, plus the picture, Cousin Jenny could do nothing but admit it. Admit it, and withdraw. Miss' Sophy's land was now her own, as it should be.

But Anders had been killed, certainly, because something had put him on this very track.

Did it mean, then, that Cousin Jenny had been the person who had brought up Sunset Joe Grenada and his killer companions?

This was hard for Ferrine to believe. This was one of the things that dissatisfied him.

Everything was all worked out, and still nothing was worked out.

The Half Circle S — what was its part in all this?

CHAPTER
TEN

"Don't they miss you back home in S-burg?" said Lumsden. "Don't they ever need a sheriff there?"

"Of course they need a sheriff there. Who would sit behind that desk and play solitaire eighteen hours a day?" said Ferrine.

Through the window, in the lazy sunlight down on court square this morning, he could see a few small birds dusting themselves, a dog sleeping, and two old men on a bench. One of them had a hickory cane at his shoulder, rifle fashion, aiming it rapidly here and there at nothing, yanking an imaginary lever, ejecting imaginary cartridge cases, all the time swerving his body this way and that, and jerking his seat up and down on the bench. All the time he kept up an excited monologue with his companion, recounting a long forgotten Indian raid, Ferrine was certain. His companion, head back on the bench, was slumbering.

"That's what they told me," said Lumsden. "But you gotta admit it's hard to believe."

"Not for me."

"Well, you was there. Would you confirm it?"

"Run through it again," said Ferrine.

Sheriff Lumsden lit one of his thick sticky cigars, and squeaked back in his chair. "It was Mr. Opperson that brought me the story, and when I questioned all the Half Circle S hands they all okayed it. Mr. Opperson hisself wasn't there, it seems. It was a crazy kind of a accident that wouldn't happen once in a million years. The Half Circle S foreman, Hackberry Tibbs, was out behind the barn — you and him had just rode in on the Half Circle S plantation wagon from Harrington. Miss' Sophy come up in her buckboard offering for sale a .45-75-305 that belonged to T. L., which she had no use for, didn't even know how to load. Hackberry, prankin' her, grabbed it and ran. It went off. And killed him. Do you confirm that?"

"You should have seen the blood," said Ferrine. "It looked like —"

"No need to go into detail," said Lumsden hastily. "I never much cared for details of that nature."

"Miss' Sophy and I left about then," said Ferrine. "What did they do with his body after we'd gone?"

"They interred it."

"I didn't care for him," said Ferrine. "But I wouldn't have wished a fate like that on him."

"Interred means buried."

"I thought you said barbecued. Since that horse threw me, like I explained, and I got this bad lip in the shake-up, I don't seem to hear too well. About this Powder River syndicate up north that owns the Half Circle S, you wouldn't happen to recall its name?"

"The Lodestone Cattle Company, or some such like."

"I wonder who owns *it?*"

"Some group of anonymous men, I'd say, or even a combination of other companies, maybe. High finance is very tricky and difficult to untangle."

"Nevertheless, I'm curious," said Ferrine. "I think I'll stop at the County Clerk's office on my way out and look at some records and maybe some tax receipts."

"They won't help," said Lumsden.

"I guess you're right," said Ferrine, who knew that this was true.

He walked to the door. "The taxes are paid by Mr. Opperson," said Lumsden. "And he'd know as little about the wheels within the wheels as you or me. He's just their local manager."

Ferrine left the courthouse and turned down Main Street, toward Trenchard's. He wanted a little more information about Opperson, and Trenchard might well be able to give it to him if he handled it right, sort of come into the subject from the side. Part way down Main, he passed the little island in the middle of the road with the depot on it and saw Henry, sagging black cotton stockings, shell-like little starched skirt, just standing in the sunlight, lonesome looking, gawking. He called, "See you later," and waved; she waved back. Trenchard, fastidiously immaculate, watching the passersby benignly, was on the bench by his door. He moved over as Ferrine approached, and Ferrine dropped down beside him.

"I see you just sitting here watching the population," said Ferrine. "Are you a lover of mankind?"

"I wish I could say I was," said Trenchard, grinning. "But I'm afraid I was just estimating their hides' hooves and tallow in dollars, cents and mills."

"That sounds pretty hardhearted," said Ferrine.

"Not hardhearted. No heart at all. Heartless."

When Ferrine made no response, Trenchard said, "And happy. Can you say the same?"

"No."

"What happened to your lip? Bee-stung?"

"Fist-stung."

"I hope you killed the man."

"I didn't, but somebody else will, later. About this Texas Slim, Mr. Trenchard, how did you happen to hire him in the first place? I hear he came to you recommended by Mr. Opperson, that he was an ex-hand or something at the Half Circle S."

"Where did you ever hear such a story?"

"At the barbershop, I think."

"He fell out of a boxcar, drunk, one night. I gave him a handful of crackers, a can of sardines, and a job next morning."

"I wouldn't think that was the best way in the world to hire labor," said Ferrine. "And I wonder how Mr. Opperson's name popped up."

"Any name will pop up in a barbershop," said Trenchard. "From Nebuchadnezzar to Nougat."

"Who the hell is Nougat?"

"Poodle. Madam Yvette's, south of the railroad tracks."

"Changing the subject from Nougat back to Mr. Opperson," said Ferrine. "How well do you know him?"

"Pretty well, I'd say. And he doesn't like to be discussed behind his back. If you've any questions about him, why don't you ask him face to face?"

"No matter," declared Ferrine. "I was just going to say —"

"We weren't going to say anything. Remember?"

"Mr. Trenchard," said Ferrine very softly. "I've just had a few very rough days. I'm short-tempered. Please don't try to teach me good manners."

Trenchard backed up so quick it was startling. It was a new Trenchard. He said, "Don't take it that way. I didn't mean it that way. Excuse me. It's *you* who could teach *me* good manners."

"Well, anyways, I could try," said Ferrine good-humoredly. "And I almost did."

He stretched upward to his feet.

"Don't go away mad," said Trenchard, looking a little harried.

"And don't tell me how or how not to go away," said Ferrine patiently, again in control of himself. "Just forget it."

There was a feedstore next door, and here he selected three corncobs from the pile on the floor by the shelling machine, pretty good ones. Next, at a nearby shop, he bought six dainty ladies' handkerchiefs, each of a different color — rose, lavender, pale green, sky blue, magenta, and white.

Henry, the stationmaster's little daughter, her spindly legs standing knock-kneed, her tight little face shining greasily, glared at him in adoration as he came up to her.

108

She said, "Deserted your wife yet?"

"Not yet," said Ferrine.

"Still hitched, but still payin' me visits on the sly, hey?"

"I brought you a present," he said, and handed her the corncobs.

"Why, thanks," she said. "They'll make dandy pipes. Bring anything to smoke in 'em?"

"You're not going to smoke them," he said. "You're going to make dolls out of them. Corncob dolls. Like your mother used to make when she was a girl. Your father can show you how."

"No dolls for me. I'm a tomboy. Tomboys' inclinations runs otherwise."

"Such as what?"

"Such as carbines and saddles and half-broke mustangs."

"Ho-hum," said Ferrine. "Last chance. Yes or no?"

"Yes," she said, taking them. "This will be Billy the Kid, this Cole Younger, and this will be John Wesley Hardin."

"They're going to look funny," he said. "Here are their dresses."

He took from his pocket the handful of gorgeous handkerchiefs.

For an instant, she just stood there, frozen.

Her eyes misted as she took them from him, very lovingly.

"They're the most beautiful things I ever saw," she said, almost mumbling it.

Gone was the tomboy. Now she was only a happy little girl.

"I have to leave now," he said. "Be a good girl, not a bad boy."

She said, "They was another of those telegrams to Theba sent last week. To a Joseph Grenada. It said, *Come again. Ride hard. Same price. Same helpers.*"

"Signed with a scribble."

"No, signed Eagle Tail Scanlon."

"What did he look like?" asked Ferrine, jarred.

"Just left on the counter, when me and my old man was out."

Another six-gun fiesta, thought Ferrine. *And this one could be for me.*

He smiled in relief, and walked away.

Back on Main Street, he paused in an alley mouth, took out the old photograph, and studied it again. With the same result: nothing. He concentrated, tried tricks with his eyes, tried everything. But he couldn't be sure whether or not he'd ever seen this man in his life. In the first place, it was too cloudy. In the second place, a man himself can change a lot in ten years.

The proper thing for him to do at this stage, he knew, was to talk it all over with Sheriff Lumsden. But that would bring on such a muddle, such long-winded criticism, that he couldn't even bear to think of it. Burt Anders would have been a real help.

Out of the corner of his eye, he saw a woman turn into a dingy little cubbyhole of a shop. Archway lettering above its door said: DRUGSTORE, SUNDRIES. The woman was lank, middle-aged, hard of jaw, and garbed in a gray dress that was almost, but not quite, a nurse's uniform. It was none other than Jennifer Johnson, Miss Cloud, Mrs. Cloud, Mrs. Eagle Tail Scanlon: Cousin Jenny. Cousin Jenny, the midwife and home remedy herbalist of Harrington — Cousin Jenny, the hub of all this trouble.

Ferrine wheeled in his step and followed her inside.

His first idea was to show her the photograph, his second was that the time for that was not yet.

She was standing at the counter, talking to the studious looking druggist behind it. Her back was to Ferrine. She was unaware of his entry.

She bought some croton oil and some ipecac.

Ipecac would make you vomit; croton oil would act on your bowels, even worse than castor oil.

So that was one of her methods. If her friends or acquaintances didn't have anything wrong, she made them think they had something wrong with them by slipping a little disturber into their tea or coffee. That would put them in a good frame of mind for her herbs.

She turned, the articles in her hand in a twist of paper, and confronted him. She recognized him instantly. She said, "If you've got anything to say, let's say it outside." Her inflection made it a command.

A few paces down the sidewalk they stopped in a doorway. She said crisply, "All right. What?"

"I didn't want to say anything," declared Ferrine. "I just stopped in there for a mustard plaster. I took it you wanted to speak to *me*."

"Well, I don't. Not now or anytime. Goodbye."

"Seen Eagle Tail lately?" he asked.

111

His question left her completely undisturbed. For an instant, he had the feeling that his trip south had been nothing but a dream, that it hadn't happened at all.

She said, "Eagle Tail? I don't know any Indians."

"This isn't an Indian. His name is Scanlon. He's your real husband, isn't he, Mrs. Scanlon?"

"I'm a widow. My husband was the late T. L. Cloud. My lawyer told me not to discuss this. Let me by, or I'll call the law."

It almost worked, he almost stepped back. He could imagine how good old Sheriff Lumsden could foul this up.

He said, "Drop this case against Miss' Sophy, Mrs. Scanlon. It doesn't have a chance."

He didn't mention the ring, or the baby's grave behind the barn, or the old woman in the adobe hotel. He didn't want the grave demolished, and the old woman visited by murderous night riders.

"Let me tell you something," she said maliciously. "It's *her* that doesn't stand a chance. I got Bible, and marriage certificate, and my lawyer tells me that's proof in any court of law. And I'll have witnesses."

"The preacher and his wife from that little Colorado town?" said Ferrine. "And by the way, what was the name of that town?"

"My lawyer will give it at the right time and place. And about witnesses — Reverend Clifford, who did the wedlocking, and his wife — they'll be there if it's possible to get them."

Neither spoke for a moment or two.

112

Finally, she said venomously, "It'll be a good trial, anyways, especially for the men folks."

He didn't ask her what she meant, but she told him because nothing could stop her. "My lawyer is going to get her up there and ask her to tell in plain everyday words just what a common-law woman is. How she beds down with a man without no sanctity at all. He's going to ask her the difference between a common-law woman and a parlor house woman. He's going to ask her why she and T. L. never had no children. He's going to ask her what she did, if anything. He's going to ask her the worst kind of doctor questions, and then pretend he didn't hear her answers, and make her say it all two or three times. My guess is that she'll have to be helped from the courtroom when it's all over."

"You aim to ruin her."

"I aim to ruin her."

"And you don't even know her, do you?"

"No, and don't want to."

"Even if she wins the case, she'll have to leave the country."

"She sure will."

"And her land will go for a song. You'll win either way."

"My lawyer said not to discuss it."

She pushed past him and strode malignantly away.

CHAPTER
ELEVEN

The man who touched him lightly on the shoulder said, "Why, it's Mr. Sheriff Bill Ferrine, of S-burg. Good to see you, sir."

Ferrine moved his head. It was Mr. Opperson himself, Land & Stock, the Big Man of Harrington. "I saw you from down the street. I thought it was you, but I wasn't sure. I'm in town on a little cattle business." In the bright sunlit street, he looked even more beast than before — arrogant, meaty, rough-pouched under the eyes. He seemed to be trying hard not to be hostile.

"Too bad about Hackberry Tibbs, out at the Half Circle S," said Ferrine.

"A man like that will be hard to replace," said Opperson, sadly shaking his head.

"But I bet you'll find someone," said Ferrine.

Opperson said, "Wasn't that Cousin Jenny, my townswoman, I saw you talking to just now?"

"It was," said Ferrine. "I'm glad I ran into you. I just came from the courthouse. Didn't do any good. Maybe you can help me."

"Be glad to, if I can. In what way?"

"Who owns Half Circle S?"

"A Powder River company up north. Called the Lodestone."

"Own a lot of other ranches?"

"Frankly, no."

"Just the Half Circle S?"

"This is confidential, but yes."

"I was talking to Sheriff Lumsden and he was saying these syndicates and companies can be pretty mixed up and tangled and hard to unravel. Have you any idea who owns the Lodestone?"

Looking smug, Mr. Opperson said, "I do."

"*You do!*"

"You've got to start somewhere. I've got big plans for it."

"Manager *and* owner," said Ferrine.

"It has its advantages," said Opperson. "To get back to Cousin Jenny. She looked excited." She had looked anything but excited. "I wonder what was troubling her?"

"You mean you wonder what we were talking about?"

"Well, yes, naturally, of course. I wondered if there was anything I could do to help."

"She was talking about her upcoming law suit," said Ferrine.

"Say, wasn't that a surprise? Not his sister but his wife. Imagine Cousin Jenny suing anybody."

When Ferrine made no response, Opperson said, "Poor lonely woman, married all the time, but just sitting out there keeping a stiff upper lip and never telling anyone about her tragedy."

"Sitting out there with her bloody abortions and filthy home remedies," said Ferrine. "She turns my stomach. I wonder what she'll do when it hits her."

"What hits her?"

"The avalanche."

"I don't understand."

"She wasn't married to T. L. Cloud, unless illegally, which I doubt. She was married to another man entirely, years ago." He took the photograph from his pocket. "This man. Known in those days as Eagle Tail Scanlon. Ever see him?"

Opperson peered.

After a moment of close study, he said, "No. What makes you think she's married to this man? Have you any other proof?"

"Plenty."

"What do you mean, plenty?"

"I can deliver the preacher that married them," said Ferrine.

It was a powerful lie, but if Cousin Jenny could wave it around, why couldn't he do the same?

Opperson's lower jaw swung over to one side, and froze there.

After a minute, he said, "I find that difficult to believe."

"Life is full of surprises, isn't it?" said Ferrine.

Opperson, backing a little but just a little, said, "For the sake of argument, and argument alone, say you're right. Say she is trying to run a little maneuver and knock off a few dollars — though I can't and won't believe it. I don't get what you said about an avalanche hitting her. If she fails, she fails, and that's all there is to it. She tried it and it didn't work. Nobody wins, nobody loses."

"Somebody loses, all right," said Ferrine.

"You mean Miss' Sophy? You mean she loses her reputation? That will all pass in time."

"I didn't mean Miss' Sophy. I'm not thinking of Miss' Sophy. Miss' Sophy can't do anything but gain by it. When it's all over, she'll be wading in money."

Opperson looked puzzled.

Ferrine said, "I'm talking about her counter-suit. The money she'll make out of that slander suit she'll follow up with."

"Oh, I don't think she'd do anything like that."

"She sure will. For one thing, I'll see that she does. It could cost Cousin Jenny every penny she has to her name, and this Scanlon, too."

"It could never come to that," Opperson said.

"In a slander case, everyone involved is guilty," said Ferrine. "And does the law really bear down on them, and squeeze them dry! Which is exactly as it should be."

He started down the walk toward the courthouse. He wanted another talk with Sheriff Lumsden.

Opperson just stood there, motionless. Looking mean and fleshy.

Never once had he said, "How do you know this Scanlon, if there was a Scanlon, isn't dead? How do you know he didn't die *after* Cousin Jenny had married him, if she did, and *before* she married T. L.? If she did marry T. L., and I think she did. That would make her

117

marriage to T. L. legal, and her case against the common-law woman sound."

He hadn't brought this up because he was sure Scanlon *had* married her, and was still alive. And assumed Ferrine had good proof of it.

But by his very silence on this point, Opperson had the same as included himself in the ugly affair.

Sheriff Lumsden was not at the courthouse later that evening; they gave Ferrine directions on how to find his home.

The little buttery-yellow house sat on a street corner between two weedy vacant lots. It had shutters and its front yard was enclosed by a whitewashed picket fence. It was immaculately kept, windowpanes gleaming, curtains snowy, and in the center of the front lawn — if there had been a lawn instead of sere grassroots — was a bed of straggly flowers circled decoratively by a wagon rim. A woman opened the door to him when he knocked.

She was sparrowlike, middle-aged, with enormous glasses and a very sweet smile.

"I'm Sheriff Bill Ferrine, of S-burg," said Ferrine. "Is Sheriff Lumsden in? I'd like to speak to him."

"He's out in the back country, serving a summons in a pig theft case," she said. "I'm Mrs. Lumsden, as you gentlemen in the profession say, his ball and chain."

"You don't say it in my house unless you want to commit suicide," said Ferrine. "Do you think I could talk to you instead?"

"Certainly," she answered. "Come in."

118

She led him into the hall, into a parlor, shuttered and in semi-darkness, and seated him. "Something on the stove. Excuse me," she said, and left. The parlor was formal, layered with stale dry air; he wondered if it had been used since its last funeral.

Mrs. Lumsden returned and seated herself. "Had to be stirred. Oxtail soup for my husband's supper. 'No bay leaves, Sarah.' What he don't know won't hurt him. 'What makes this so good, Sarah?' Careful braising, it's all in the braising. Now what can I do for you?"

"Have you lived long hereabouts, Mrs. Lumsden?"

"Hereabouts all of my life, about. We came to Farley shortly after the railroad. My father was a failure. A jack-of-all-failures, you might say. But his specialty was cattle raising failures. That was where he pulled off his finest ones. So we moved to town where he could talk about them. It's no fun having failures if there's no one but your family to listen to them."

"Ever know of a man called Eagle Tail Scanlon?"

"Not that I recall. The Irish track-workers were mostly gone when we got here."

"This man wasn't likely a track-worker. What do you know of the Half Circle S?"

"We lived on a small place nigh there once when I was a girl, when my father was working at his trade of ranch failures." She seemed to be engulfed in memory for an instant, then shook it off. "The Half Circle S. Once it was considered as crooked as a dog's hind leg, but that's all changed."

Ferrine asked, "How do you know it's changed?"

"New ownership, new people, for one thing. For another, no more complaints from neighbors. You can't fool your near-neighbors when you're running a place that's out of kilter."

Through the house, from the front door, they heard a hollow knock. Mrs. Lumsden got up, left the room, and returned with a man. He was short, droopy-eyed, unshorn, and wore skintight, hide-legging chaps, denim work pants ballooning out at their seat. He held his hat respectfully at his chest, because he was inside a real home, and was excited. He impressed Ferrine as a man that spent his life in the open.

He said, "Your husband done me a favor once, Mrs. Lumsden. I want to repay it. This-here's that chance. I got to see him."

Mrs. Lumsden said graciously, "But like I told you, he's not here. He's out in the back country, serving a summons."

"This needs lawing," said the man.

"What's the trouble?" asked Ferrine.

"Who are you?" asked the vistor.

"Bill Ferrine, sheriff at S-burg."

"Sheriff?" said the man. "Then you'll have to take care of it."

"Not unless I have to," said Ferrine. "It's been carefully explained to me that I'm outside my franchise. What's happening?"

"The bartender at the Crescent Saloon sent me," said the man. "They's four strangers in his back room."

"And what's so special about that?" asked Ferrine.

120

"He claims they is the same ones that gunned down Burt Anders. That he was there and seen it when it happened. That they're back."

"Let's go," said Ferrine. His voice was childlike and gentle.

Mrs. Lumsden went with them to the doorstep. The man started down the brick walk toward the gate.

Mrs. Lumsden said quickly, "I don't know him. In spite of all his easy-sounding Mrs. Lumsden this and Mrs. Lumsden that, I don't know him. Leave it be."

"After I worked this hard to make it happen?" said Ferrine.

CHAPTER
TWELVE

His nameless companion was waiting at the gate for him, holding it open encouragingly, almost seeming to be trying to draw him out and along by magnetism. "Beautiful night," said Ferrine. "I see there's a ring around the moon. My grandmother used to say that on nights like this rosebuds leaned over in their gardens and kissed each other. You ever hear that one?"

"No," said the man, startled. "And if I did hear it, I sure wouldn't pass it on. You certain you're Bill Ferrine, the sheriff?"

"What makes you doubt it?"

"You don't scarcely ever hear sheriffs talking that way."

"Sheriffs are human like anyone else," said Ferrine.

"If you can call that human." They lapsed into silence.

Ferrine had noticed the Crescent Saloon several times. It was one of the sun-blistered false-fronted buildings in the forlorn rectangle of offices and stores and barrooms that enclosed the courtsquare, about midway in the row that faced the front of the courthouse. Its window glass had been painted black two-thirds of the way up on the inside. There was a downspout by its door, and a barrel under the spout to catch any precious rain; in the bottom of the barrel there was about an inch of thick green scum. It seemed a wretched looking place, and, to Ferrine, gave off a feeling of being quietly and definitely sinister. If the bartender had been at his door when Anders had been killed in the square, he could have seen the shooting plainly.

The night was black. Downtown, only a few shops showed nightlights, and those weakly. They were passing Trenchard's store, closed and shadowy, when Ferrine said, "This is far enough for you. There's going to be fireworks."

"I'm coming along," said the man. "I told you I was beholden to Sheriff Lumsden, and it could be you could use another gun."

"Who are you, by the way?" said Ferrine. "And how come you're so beholden to Sheriff Lumsden?"

"I don't feel free to go into it," said the man. "I'll leave Lumsden explain it later if he wants. To get back to this other. I've got a plan. Would you care to hear it?"

"Why not?" said Ferrine. "Tell me." He came to a stop. The man halted in front of him.

"It's this," said the man in a hoarse whisper. "Like I said, they're in the back room. You borrow an apron and a tray from the barman out front and go in, like you made a mistake. You can have your gun out and under your apron. Man, will they look foolish! I'll be right behind you."

"We'll do it just that way," said Ferrine. "I can hardly wait."

He took out his gun, bringing it to full cock in the same flow of movement, and laid it flat along the man's jawline, cylinder, barrel, and muzzle.

It must have seemed cold.

The man's eyes went egg-white shiny and his lips moved soundlessly.

Ferrine said, "How many men did you say? Four?"

The man managed to nod, stiffly.

"I think three," said Ferrine. "I think you're the fourth. The bait. The man that walks behind me."

With great muscular difficulty, the man said, "No."

Ferrine said quietly, "Burt Anders was my friend."

The man's eyes seemed fixed now, almost sightless in their glow of terror.

"How many helpless men you shot down in your day?" asked Ferrine. "Three? Nine?"

The man simply stood there.

Ferrine said, "You're a pro, aren't you? Why don't you draw. Why don't you say to hell with this and go down trying?"

The man shook his head.

Ferrine said, "You've got a chance. If you talk. If you talk *and* I believe you as you go along."

"Why not?" said the man. "I'm dead anyway. Like you say, I'm one of Sunset's boys, the fourth, and burnt my powder along with the others when Anders was killed. They're at the Crescent, waiting for you. I was to bring you in."

"Why was Anders wanted dead?"

"He was messin' around."

"And me?"

"Same reason. Too much. Something about a marriage, I think."

"Who ordered and paid for it?"

"I couldn't say. I just ride and shoot and follow instructions."

Ferrine said, "And you stay at the Half Circle S when you're in this part of ths country?"

"We done so twice. This time and the other."

"Know any Eagle Tail Scanlon?"

"Heard of him. Never saw him. He was before my day."

"Where is he now?"

"No idea."

That would be the way it would be handled. No one would know but Sunset Joe Grenada.

"I'm not going to kill you," said Ferrine, slamming the man, hard, at the base of his neck with his six-gun. "Because I believe you, and try to be a man of my word." The man slumped inertly to the walk. Ferrine took handcuffs from the small of his back and clipped the man to a stanchion. "I hereby assign you officially to Chairman Lumsden." He took the man's gun, removed its cartridges, carried the weapon a short way with him into an alley and tossed it into a trash-box.

One thing about Lumsden, Ferrine reflected. If he didn't come right out and beg for trouble here in Farley, he did about the next thing to it. When he left town, he certainly advertised his departure. Sunset Joe and his friends must have known about it, down to its last detail. They'd constructed their entire deadfall for Ferrine around his absence.

When this alley was crossed by another, he turned right, down the second alley. Now he began counting back doors, some scarcely discernible in the blackness. There were windows, too, most back maws in the night, occasionally one blooming with golden lamplight, from a shopkeeper totaling up his books, or from a saloon back room, or from a pool hall. Farley's night-collectors of garbage were around him as he walked, rats, dogs, cats, formless shadows fluttering around his ankles, rustling in paper, scratching and clawing.

Then, before him, was the beam of lamplight which was his destination. He was pretty sure it was from the back window of the Crescent Saloon.

He approached it carefully. It was curtained by a bedsheet tacked to its inside frame.

He inspected the door beside the window. It could be barred within, or bolted, or simply locked. If it was barred, he was out of luck.

He stepped back, drew his gun, and gave the door a tremendous stamping smash with his heel using calf, thigh, and backbone in the impact.

There was no bar.

The door flew open, the mortise-tongue of the lock crashing the door frame inward in splinters.

He followed his action inside, half rolling to keep his balance.

There were four men at a table, half turned from him, watching a closed door to the front of the saloon.

Four, not three as he had expected.

The fourth man was Trenchard, the store owner.

Trenchard was Eagle Tail Scanlon, Ferrine realized.

He was in serious trouble, and was here in person to see that the job was completely successful.

They had drawn guns in their hands, all four of them.

Ferrine said curtly, "Don't move." Then added invitingly, "Unless, of course, you want to."

They pivoted their heads very slowly in his direction. Trenchard was just as Ferrine had first seen him that day in the store, tall and serene, garbed in fine light brown wool, sparkling with gold at cuff links and collar button. His black Stetson was on the table in front of him. His brown-blotched, almost bald skull shone with droplets of sweat.

On his left sat a little creature of a man, pointed face, snarl-lifted lips, needle teeth, who put Ferrine in mind of a possum, and on his right, a big lumpish mortal in khaki, sun-florid, with cruel slippery black eyes. Directly across from him was the gunman who had to be Sunset Joe Grenada, brighter than all the others except Trenchard, fastidiously clean in store-new clothes and a beaded vest, pitted on the ball of his chin and about the corners of his eyes with relics of old Apache smallpox, likely, level-eyed and half amused. A high caliber man in his manner, and probably very high caliber in his marksmanship.

These friends of Trenchard's were professionals, who had probably picked up a gun before they had picked up a razor. Their looks confirmed the feeling that had been growing on Ferrine: at one time Eagle Tail Scanlon had likely been a professional himself.

Still in the crouch from his lunge, Ferrine said, "You've come a long way, Eagle Tail. No Mexican bangles and new manners."

"That's right," said Trenchard. "New everything. Which includes property, legal, a heap of it, and still growing."

"But the same old legal wife," said Ferrine.

"Why couldn't you and Burt Anders leave well enough alone?" asked Trenchard.

They sat rigid.

The man in khaki said, "Where's Bucky? You shoot him?"

"If he's the man you sent for me," said Ferrine, "he's in the custody of Sheriff Lumsden."

"Lumsden is out in the back country serving a paper," said Trenchard.

"Is he?" said Ferrine. "Well, that's fine."

"Watch it," said Sunset Joe. "He's trying to spook us into action, into sudden death. I have a feeling this man is good."

"One against four?" said Trenchard desperately. "Not that good."

"You're the man that pays the bills," said Sunset Joe, and whipped up with a snapshot.

Ferrine nailed him upward, in the left eye, before his gun had half circled.

Trenchard, seeing his world collapse, crazy, tried to rush in tandem, and got his, two laid carefully into his heart.

"Next?" said Ferrine. "Now you got two against one, gentlemen, and that's better odds than flipping coins."

128

The possum faced man said, "I'm laying down my gun. I don't want to die" — and tried it himself. Ferrine blasted him half out of his chair, a-sprawl across the tabletop.

The big man in khaki said reasonably, "He had to take a chance. You can only hang once, and they's too many posses after him right now." He spread his fingers and his weapon dropped to the floor. "You wouldn't shoot an unarmed man!"

"They're the best kind," said Ferrine. "Anders didn't have a chance."

"But I'm just a country boy," blurted the man. "Who fell amongst evil companions. I want to get back to that good old plow and that good old scythe." He was about fifty years old.

"I bet you do," said Ferrine. He made a quick decision. He said, "Okay. Come along."

He thought, *All the gunshots, and never an appearance from anyone out front. I'll remember that. The bartender was in on it, too.*

As they left by the alley, the big man said, "I don't think I'm going to enjoy it, if they hang me."

"You'll get used to it," said Ferrine. "And they might not hang you, just give you thirty or forty years."

"I'd love that worse," said the man. "The penitentiary."

"You can always break out," said Ferrine.

CHAPTER
THIRTEEN

The window blinds were up in the Lumsden parlor; outside, the day had gone into gloaming, and Mrs. Lumsden had lit two kerosene lamps, her best ones, with strands of green and red glass beads on their shades. Now she was passing around a picnic supper of fried chicken, deviled eggs, cornbread sticks, potato salad, and warty little sweet pickles. It was two weeks after the shoot-out at the Crescent, and there was an air of festivity. Miss' Sophy Cloud had married her top-hand, Mr. Layton. Present were the bridal pair, the boy Tolliver, Sheriff Lumsden and Ferrine.

"How did you come to do it?" asked Lumsden.

Miss' Sophy said, "I thought it was about time somebody made an honest man of him."

"I wasn't talking to you," said Lumsden. "I was addressin' your spouse."

"She come beggin' and crawlin' and makin' these horrible moans, and my judgment slipped me for an instant and I said yes," replied Mr. Layton. "Ain't that the way everybody does it?"

"Do you regret it?" asked Ferrine.

"Yes," said Layton. "A husband works harder than a top-hand."

130

"I hope you got the papers to prove it," said Ferrine.

"We got enough papers to wrap seventeen pounds of pork-chops," said Layton. "Not only that, we got the preacher chained in the root cellar."

Miss' Sophy said, "You gentlemen can go too far with this-here."

Tolliver said, "I like them little pickles, Mrs. Lumsden."

Mrs. Lumsden said, "They ain't much, I'm afraid." She blushed. "Though the Mister likes them."

"She can't habit herself to say 'sheriff,'" said Lumsden. "She was the same way with 'chairman.'"

He munched a chicken thigh, and said, "They was a reward on one of them fellows, Sheriff Ferrine. I aim to split it with you halfway, even-steven."

"Give my part to Henry," said Ferrine. "Without Henry, we couldn't have done it."

"Who is Henry?" asked Tolliver. "How about another handful of that salad?"

"The stationmaster's daughter," said Ferrine. "And if she throws it back in your face, just walk away and leave it. She has her own way of doing things. She'll pick it up. She needs it."

"So Trenchard was really the Lodestone syndicate?" said Miss' Sophy.

"That's right," said Ferrine. "He owned the Half Circle S. Opperson was just his manager out there. He owned the Crescent Saloon, too. Along with a lot of other Farley property."

"What's goin' on out at Half Circle S that shouldn't be goin' on?" asked Mr. Layton.

"Nothing, as far as I could tell," said Ferrine.

"Then why did they stir up so much trouble agin us?" asked Tolliver. "Where did my chicken salad go?"

"The terrible thing," said Lumsden, "is where did the bone to your chicken thigh go?"

"They caused all this mess for one purpose, and one purpose only," said Ferine. "They wanted your place, Miss' Sophy. It adjoined theirs."

"That's my opinion, too," said Mr. Layton.

"It's not opinion, it's fact," said Ferrine. "Opperson has said so."

"I wonder why Burt Anders was killed," said Miss' Sophy. "I liked him."

"Opperson says he ran into an old wanted poster that said an Eagle Tail Scanlon, a stage robber, had an alias of Trenchard, and asked Trenchard about it."

"Opperson here, too?" asked Mr. Layton.

"He's tied down his throttle," said Lumsden. "You should listen to him."

"You don't see no bones on my plate, Sheriff Lumsden, because these-here nice little pickles don't have no bone. It ain't in the nature of pickles to have bones," said Tolliver patiently.

Miss' Sophy said, "I'm goin' to take him after a bit, Sheriff Lumsden. So they ain't no need to go poppin' your eyes and working your mouth, and gettin' all set trying to untangle it. You know what I was thinkin' about? Eagle Tail Scanlon. When he deserted his wife, Cousin Jenny, down south there at that adobe hotel, if he'd have wound up at some other place he might still be alive."

"I doubt it. Or sooner dead, I'd say," said Ferrine.

132

"How did Mr. Cloud ever get that receipt in his strong-box?" asked Miss' Sophy. "You said it was a fake."

"It was a fake, just written out then, for the time and place. When Hackberry Tibbs and Texas Slim visited you that day, whilst you were out with Hackberry on a wild goose chase, Texas Slim, stayin' back, took the opportunity of putting it in the strongbox. That was why they really came to your place, of course."

"They could have did it as you say," answered Miss' Sophy. "Mr. Cloud hadn't really had any carryings-on with this Harrington woman, had he?"

"He hadn't ever seen her, and had never even heard of her," said Ferrine.

"That makes me feel better," said Miss' Sophy.

"Don't everybody stare at me when she says that," said Mr. Layton. "I ain't got a jealous element in my body. In Miss' Sophy's previous cases of the heart, I'm just her old top-hand again."

Ferrine said, "And Texas Slim was sent to the rooming house to kill me because they were beginning to worry about me."

"Well, he didn't pull it off," said Layton. "And later, when they were really scared of you, they brought Sunset Joe up once more and tried it on you."

"That's the way I figure it," said Ferrine.

"Scared of you," said Sheriff Lumsden. Reproachfully, he asked, "Why isn't anyone scared of me?"

"I bet the man you served that pig theft summons on was scared of you," said Ferrine encouragingly.

"And I'm scared of him," said Mrs. Lumsden soothingly.